THE GREAT LAZARUS

by
RED SKELTON

Red Skelton

My thanks to Donald A. Seybold for his encouragement and to the Great Lazarus for living such a colorful life.

CHAPTER ONE

It was rather chilly for the month of April, but the little town of Greensville knew it was spring because the carnival was in town and the citizens were making ready for the Easter festival. The advent of spring was reason enough for these townspeople to celebrate. There seemed to be a rainbow and Greensville was the pot at its end. There would be a parade with various organizations, marching bands, the Shrine clowns and the de Moley, a highly respected Masonic group of young men who had better things to do than participate in vandalism. They wanted to serve a purpose, not contribute to mindless destruction.

Even so, the welcome sign was riddled with bullet holes, and there were hate signs written on fences—things such as: "Jesus saves; Moses Invests." Most of the rocks and boulders, and the walls of empty buildings had been defaced with graffiti. The lazy and the ignorant had scrawled their social, political, sexual, and obscene messages everywhere. Fortunately, most of the messages were illiterate and misspelled and revealed the stupidity of the authors.

But at festival time the visitors poured in from the neighboring towns, filling the hotels and rooming houses. They came for the beauty here that overcomes the ugliness. The peach and apple trees are in full blossom. Shrubs are dressed in large clusters of white and pale reddish purple flowers. Flowers sway fragrantly in the gentle breeze. You could almost hear a thousand little bells tinkling, were it not for the noise of the students and their guests home on vacation.

1

The queen of the carnival has been selected from the local college, a small one some call *The Frankie and Johnny*. It's sort of a low-brow *William and Mary*. The Queen will arrive in a golden coach drawn by six white horses, which are so old that a tractor will have to be brought in to pull the coach back to its starting point. This royal coach was built in 1800 and is only used for this event. At noon there will be a luncheon and the ceremonial opening of the festival, which is the same every year, except for the new queen and her court of ladies-in-waiting. A couple of her ladies appear to have been waiting for a long time. The queen will display some outstanding talent that I've never been able to sit through. Some sing, some dance; others, in the past, have played harp, violin or piano. This year, as always, the queen will be introduced by some local politician who has never met the young lady before. But he will predict that her beauty and talent will take her to great heights, should she adopt a theatrical career as her lifetime work. All the ex-queens will be present with their memories of the same flattering remarks, still dreaming of fame, but now too busy cooking for a husband and three children to do anything but regret that they hadn't taken the flattery as encouragement and followed through on their dreams. I wonder how the flattery will affect this young queen—a new girl hearing the old words. The newspaper will praise her and predict stardom. I know. I've already written the story that will appear in tomorrow morning's edition.

Yesterday, I made a visit to the carnival location. It is exciting to see thirty-six flat cars on the side tracks of the B and O railroad, loaded with circus wagons and trailers, transformed into a portable amusement park in two hours. It is even more exciting to experience the carnival atmosphere come to life with the hot dog stands, the merry-go-round, the ferris wheel, roller coaster and the small canvas booths for the exhibits and games of skill.

I stood and listened to the pitchmen make their spiel and I watched them lean over the counter to flirt with the girls. These dandies flaunted their magnetic charm, persuading the town folks to spend ten cents to test their skill at throwing baseballs at a pyramid of wooden milk bottles in order to knock them off the pedestal and win a stuffed teddy bear or a chalk cupie doll with Clara Bow lips. A quick observation convinced me that humans are like sheep; they see a shill walking around the midway with a stuffed animal and are willing to spend four or five dollars trying to win one for the little lady when they could buy one for half that at the store. We all try to keep up with the Joneses when it is much easier to bring them down to our level, and the games of chance are the most popular gimmicks for doing so. I listened to the clacking of the Fargo Wheel, where twenty-five cents gave you a chance to win a smoked ham.

The attractions that needed the least ballyhoo were the girlie show and the side show with the odd-looking people, who, after a short novelty act of some sort, sell their photographs. Sword swallowers, magicians, a fat lady, a rubber man, a snake charmer and a human pin cushion were all part of this show. The tallest man, along with the smallest man in the world were there. One was eight feet tall, the other only three feet.

Even though it intrigued me I could never fully understand the fascination and mystery of the midway. Perhaps it was the tents containing the strange attractions and festooned with the gaudily painted banners. Some of these were 30 × 15 feet, with art work depicting what could be seen inside the tent. There was nothing subliminal about these advertisements which lured the people into paying admission to enter the hot, stuffy tents.

Being an amateur student of the art of public attractions I was curious about, in fact in love with, the midway. As I said, I don't know exactly why. Maybe it was the ferris wheel, the merry-go-round, the electric bump 'em cars, or maybe it was the cheap thrill of riding the roller coaster and not realizing the true danger of the fast moving, box-like seats-on-wheels traveling at speeds of fifty miles an hour through sharp turns and curves. The coaster was erected in two hours and might well have been missing a nut or bolt somewhere along the track. But, whatever the reason, I found myself walking around, enjoying the fragrance of fresh sawdust which will be raked up and hauled away one hour after the carnival was torn down and on its way to another city. Here in Greensville, as part of the contract with the city, the field had to be cleaned up at the close of the week.

I've always been fascinated by the eloquence of the side-show barker, each word is pure elocution. His voice echoes through the crowd like a huge bell, his basso profundo voice actually pierces the eardrum. Truly a subliminal spiel, that monotone, "Hurry! Hurry! Hurry! Fifty cents, one half dollar, see Juanita that poison spider girl from Mexico! Half girl, half spider!"

This barker looked like a gentlemen—well pressed, dressed in a gray high silk hat, gray frock coat with pearl gray vest and checkered black and white pants, not unlike those worn by butchers. He wore white spats and shiny black patent leather shoes, and had a gold watch chain with some impressive secret order's emblem dangling from the fob. His cravat sported a perfect ascot, highlighted with a huge pearl stickpin. Each hair on his head was perfectly groomed. I could never figure out how such a man could remove his hat, even on a hot day, and not leave the imprint of the hatband about his forehead, or, at least, ruffle a few hairs.

There is another mystery about barkers. The hot sun dries out the earth, creating a dust that causes an asthmatic nightmarish feeling; but regardless of the color of the earth, the barker's shoes always take on a grayish sheen, not unlike suede. It is not an uncommon sight to see men wipe the dust off their shoes by rubbing the toes against the pants at the calf of the leg, but regardless of how thick the dust, a barker's shoes are never dusty. Yet, under the closest scrutiny, I've never seen one of them rub their shoes on his calf or stoop over and polish dust from his shoes. They always look like a Shinola ad.

And still another mystery! A barker's breast pocket handkerchief is always folded so that all four corners stand like sentinels protecting a little red, white, and blue circular lapel pin. I've always wondered what the emblem represented.

I stood there listening to the barker speak from a platform flanked by two ticket booths. In front of the large tent were huge paintings depicting what could be seen on the inside. It was bad poster art, painted on thick canvas. Words passed over the barker's pearl white teeth, which seemed much whiter than normal because of his tanned skin. He was speaking in a voice that sounded like a foghorn warning passing ships of danger. "Hurry! Hurry! Hurry! The performance will start in five minutes. See a phenomenon only performed by Christ after he was tortured and pronounced dead, and then was raised from the dead. See before your eyes, one of the wonders of mankind. See The Great Lazarus die before your eyes and be pronounced dead by two of your local physicians. Then, watch him rise up and live again!"

This spiel piqued my curiosity. The portable theater was tacky, but impressive, all the same. Large, gaudy, and distasteful canvas paintings hung on both sides of the entrance. One showed a man rising out of a casket; the other depicted the ascension, including an angel with his arms outstretched, standing on a cloud. Over the entrance was the psalm, "Yea, though I walk through the valley of the shadow of death, I shall fear no evil, for thou art with me, thy rod and thy staff they comfort me."

If this is not a fraud, I thought, this has to be a very pious man rejoicing in the goodness of heaven; his heart must overflow with gratitude. If The Great Lazarus is able to die on stage and then be resurrected, his belief in good must be so strong that he has a message for the scientific and spiritual world to study. Then, I looked once again at the dirty tent filled with holes and patches. I wondered, "Is this the house of the Lord! Or is it only because of the money that he will dwell there forever!"

5

Was it a gimmick? Did he even approach the shadow of death? There has to be something to guard him from such a dark, perilous region. But suppose he doesn't return to life after the doctor pronounces him dead? Who cares except the three hundred people clamoring for their money back?

I bought my ticket out of curiosity, hoping I would find something fraudulent. I was ready to expose this charlatan, but, this being the Bible belt, I'm sure I wasn't the only skeptic.

The audience was mostly elderly people. There was a somber hush, a deathwatch silence as everyone paid fifty cents, perhaps hoping to discover the secret of this phenomenon so they could use it to outsmart the grim reaper.

The tent was stuffy. The body heat from over 300 people intensified the temperature, even though the back sidewall of the tent had been lowered to allow fresh air to circulate. The place was packed, all but a few were standing. In front of the stage there were ten rows of wooden folding chairs for twenty-five cents extra where people could watch the performance seated. All those reserved seats were taken. There wasn't a mumbling of voices like one would hear in a theater before the curtain. There was just a silence such as I had never before witnessed.

Just then, on stage, walking toward the footlights, came the barker. He now wore an oxford gray coat and striped pants. "Welcome," he bellowed, but in a warm, gracious manner. "Allow me to introduce myself. I am Charlie Price. I would also like you to meet two doctors who practice in your fair city. This is Dr. Handly J. Williams." The doctor walked on stage and, with no stage presence whatsover, gave a wave of the hand. There was a short, not too enthusiastic, round of applause. "And this is Dr. Fred Obliss." This pudgy, little pill peddler was more flamboyant. One look at him and you could tell his bedside manners didn't have any. He was received with polite applause. Then Mr. Price dominated the stage once again.

6

"Ladies and gentlemen, the phenomenon you are about to witness is without legerdemain, or, to put it into the words of a layman, there is no trickery or deception. The Great Lazarus will die before your eyes. These two doctors will legitimize that conclusion when The Great Lazarus has no sign of life within his body. If there are those in the audience who have legitimate credentials and are in good standing with the American Medical Association, they may feel free to examine the body.

"Sometimes this performance is such a shock to some in the audience that we have, as a precaution, stationed a registered nurse at the corner of the stage, ready to administer first aid to any who may require it."

I looked toward the nurse. She was a tall blond with wistful eyes and a curvaceous body that would prevent any man in the audience from fainting. She stood by a table with a clean, white towel covering the top. On the table was a first aid kit, bottles of smelling salts and vials of spirits of ammonia, a box of Kleenex, along with a large porcelain bowl filled with ice cubes, and a stack of white linen towels. Next to the table were two army cots, each covered with white sheets and a pillow. The nurse pointed to these articles as if she were selling them.

Then my attention returned to the stage as Mr. Price continued his speech. "I do request that you give your undivided attention to what is being presented on stage at all times. Should The Great Lazarus not rise from the dead, I hold in my hand an insurance policy naming his beneficiary as The Shrine Crippled Children's Hospital."

There was a sound of applause and a few comments of "How thoughtful!"

"Now, ladies and gentlemen, The Great Lazarus."

Ancient sounding music came from a phonograph being played backstage. Then, on stage walked this hulk of a man, who weighed about two hundred pounds. His hair was re-

7

ceding, but he had a very warm smile and ingratiating personality. He wore sandals, and a toga which reached his knees. There was a light round of applause.

Suddenly, a slight chill surged through my body. There was something saintly about his presence, a kindness and goodness. He appeared deeply concerned as he picked up a silver goblet from a small marble table beside the ancient Greecian bed. He sat down on the bed and drank from the goblet.

"Confound the weather," he said impatiently.

The two doctors took their stethoscopes and listened to his heart. Both agreed he had a strong, normal heartbeat. They moved away from the bed as The Great Lazarus spoke.

"Life's mystery will never by completely solved. Should I not be able to rise again, then I shall forever leave this empty social shell I've been born into."

He paused for a moment, then poured liquid from a container into the goblet, and shuddered as he brought the goblet to his lips. "The Lord giveth, the Lord taketh away," he said. Looking at the audience he made a wry expression, then, with a sigh of discontent, said, "Forgive my reaction to this horrible concoction, but I am sure there are many in this congregation who would also find it distasteful." He smiled, then continued, "It is H_2O, commonly referred to as water. What a splendid nightcap! It is now time to leave this life, and Lord knows how I cherish life," he muttered with a grin, as he looked to heaven. Initially, his voice was strong, then it slowly weakened as he stretched out on the bed. After a few seconds the color began to leave his face.

"I now quote Matthew 6:9–13 and Luke 11:24. 'Our father who art in heaven.' " Then he mumbled again. After a few seconds he was heard to say, " 'Yea, though I walk the valley of the shadow of death, I fear no evil.' " Then he became motionless.

There was a deadly hush. Two minutes passed, then Mr. Price stepped to the bed. With his index finger and thumb, he opened the eyes of The Great Lazarus, then closed them and summoned the doctors to examine the body. Each second became more dramatic. The two doctors, standing over the body with stethoscopes about their necks, became concerned. The first doctor leaned forward, took Lazarus' wrist in his hand, placed his index finger on the pulse and listened to The Great Lazarus' heart with the stethoscope. Bewilderment suddenly appeared on the doctor's face. He stood there, looking around, shaking his head, and, then, with a tilt of his head, he motioned the other doctor to examine the body. The second doctor leaned down and listened with his stethoscope, and bewilderment spread across his face. He looked up, helplessly and fearfully, towards the other doctor. The half smile on his face changed from smugness to concern. Nervously, he announced, "This man is dead!"

There was a gasp from the audience; some blessed themselves. One lady fainted and the nurse hurried to her and gave her a whiff of the spirits of ammonia. One doctor removed his coat and started to administer first aid, but Mr. Price stopped him.

"Please doctor, that won't be necessary," he said as he pushed the doctor away. Then he asked the other one, "Doctor, what is your verdict?"

"The man is dead."

"Are you sure?"

The first doctor shook his head and shrugged his shoulders. To make sure, he replaced the stethoscope in his ears and listened more intently. Again his eyebrows lifted as he looked up.

"Is he dead?" asked Mr. Price.

The doctor stood, looking as if he had seen a ghost. "I'd hate to be his insurance company," said the doctor, as he removed his stethoscope. He continued to shake his head, but he didn't take his eyes off the body.

The audience sat spellbound. There were sounds of sobbing. Then one voice shouted, "May God be with us all!"

Mr. Price took over as he stepped down to the footlights of

9

the makeshift stage. In a dramatic tone, he announced joyously, "Ladies and gentlemen, you have just heard the verdict of these two eminent doctors, both well-known to you, both members of the AMA, licensed to practice here in town. They have pronounced The Great Lazarus dead. How sad it would be if such a pronouncement were true, and in ordinary circumstances this diagnosis would be acceptable. It makes you wonder how many bodies have been buried while still alive." Mr. Price became reverent as he faced the audience. "Is there any skeptic with proper qualifications who cares to examine the body of this great man?"

I have a strange feeling I can't explain, like I've been at a crucifixion. I want to stand up and say, "I'm with the local press and I'd like to examine the body." But I am listless. I can't move. I sit in disbelief. And there are no other volunteers.

"Then I ask you all to have respect and remain silent for five minutes." Someone coughed. Price glared in the direction of the cough. "Absolute silence," he said with great authority.

After several minutes of silence, Price continued, "Within a few seconds you are going to see a phenomenon that has baffled medical men all over the world, and unless witnessed with your own eyes, this death would seem inconceivable. What you are about to see will haunt you for the rest of your life. For you will see this body slowly come to life."

With that spectacular statement the lights dimmed and a spotlight covered the body—a pure white spot. Ancient harp music came from off stage. It was a most dramatic sight—over three hundred strangers staring at a body that had just been proclaimed dead. In a matter of seconds, Lazarus' finger moved and then the entire hand. Slowly, his head moved from one side to the other.

There was a gasp from the audience.

Then, suddenly full of vitality, Lazarus complexion returned to normal. And, finally, with a great crescendo from the harps, The Great Lazarus sat up. He looked around, bewildered at first, then he smiled. This was followed by a gesture reminiscent of an acrobat taking a bow, slowly stretching both hands out at his sides at a forty-five degree angle. He held this pose, like a sainted statue in prayer, while he acknowledged the applause, which was slow in coming. Then he looked toward the heavens, grasped the ridge of his nose with his index finger and thumb, shook his head and left the stage as if he were completely exhausted.

Thunderous applause erupted as the curtain closed.

CHAPTER TWO

Being a news reporter, I saw a great story in Lazarus. I had to talk to him. So, filled with determination, and knowing that no one on the paper had ever interviewed a carnival person before, I took a chance, after the performance, and made my way, though uninvited, to The Great Lazarus' dressing room tent. On the way, I passed a few tough-looking groups of roustabouts (the men who put up and tear down the tents). After inquiring several different places, I located the area where his tent was pitched. There I met a rough-looking, unshaven fellow whose feet were bare. He wore pants and a dirty undershirt, and as he walked toward me, his expression was anything but friendly. He looked like a walking "No Trespassing" sign. I felt like I was approaching a revolving door with a pair of skis across my shoulders. He smelled of booze; his breath could wilt artificial flowers.

"Wacha doin' back here?"

I beamed my eyes right at him, then childlike, I adopted a cordial grin. "I have an appointment with The Great Lazarus." I was ready to concede to his wishes, whatever they were, but luckily, he pointed vaguely toward a nearby tent.

"He's in there, that's his tent."

"Thank you," I said, handing him a dollar bill. He immediately became overly polite and very British.

"Thank you, Governor," he said as he removed his cap and made a sweeping gesture as he bowed, practically falling on his face as he staggered forward. Then, regaining his balance, he gave a little hop and walked away.

I moved to the tent's entrance. The flap was open, so I looked in. The sidewalls were at half mast to allow air to circulate through the tent. There was an oriental rug covering the dirt floor, an army cot, two straightback chairs, and a folding table holding a five gallon "Ice Water" container with a spigot. In the center of the tent was a stool, on it an electric fan faced an old-fashioned wash tub with a hundred pound cake of ice in it. Seated in front of this improvised air conditioner, cooling himself with a large palm fan, sat The Great Lazarus, wearing boxer shorts. He had a Turkish bath towel draped over his lap. I knocked on a tent pole to get his attention.

He looked up and said, "Hello. Come in."

I didn't expect him to be so friendly, or so inventive. The fan blowing across the cake of ice really cooled the place very little, but any suggestion of cool air helped. There is nothing as stuffy as a canvas tent on a hot day when the sun is beaming down on it.

I extended my hand and introduced myself. "I'm Jim Lawson from the Associated Press and the Greensville Reporter."

"I am Lazarus," he said as he stood up, holding on to the towel wrapped around his middle. "Come, pull up a chair and make yourself comfortable. Take off your coat. Here, sit on this side of the ice. It cools a little."

I pulled up a folding canvas chair, took off my coat and took out my pad and pencil. I was surprised at how much younger he looked when viewed close up. He had honesty in his face, and his eyes sparkled. They seemed pixie-like. When I shook his hand it had great strength in it, yet the touch was most gentle in its firmness. He was very congenial.

He turned and addressed the nurse, who I hadn't noticed when I walked in. "Get Mr. Lawson a glass of lemonade, please."

She removed a towel that covered a glass pitcher and poured lemonade into a paper cup.

"I love lemonade, he said. "Lemonade and hot dogs." He

14

became most enthusiastic. "Would you like a hot dog? the nurse will go and get them, if you'd like one."

"No, no! The cold drink will be fine," I said.

Taking the cup from the nurse, he asked, "Ruby dear, would you go and get us some hot dogs? There is a stand just across from the main tent."

She picked up her handbag.

"Get the money out of my pants' pocket," he said nonchalantly.

Trusting soul, I thought, as she handed him his trousers.

He handed her a five dollar bill. "Get yourself a couple, if you like."

The nurse smiled. "I've got to watch my figure," she said with a little primp.

I thought, why not watch her figure? I sure did.

Lazarus sat back in his chair. "Is the lemonade sweet enough for you? There is some sugar over there. They make it a little tangy for me." He exhaled and said, "Now, what can I do for you?"

"Thank you," I said, almost in disbelief. Though I knew he was a friendly man on stage, this treatment added more mystery to him. Before I could get another word out, in walked Mr. Price, the barker. He seemed different. His vocabulary was strictly south Brooklyn. He'd lost his stage presence and his nicely perfected facade of dignity.

Lazarus introduced us. "This is Jim Lawson, from the newspaper."

The barker seemed upset. "The Great Lazarus don't give no interviews. Anything ya got ta know ya get from me," he said, not even bothering to shake my hand.

Lazarus interrupted. "What he means to say is that the reason I don't give interviews is no one has ever asked before."

"So you're from the press? My name is Price—P R I C E! Charlie Price, that is. I handle all the press. I own the show." He took off his coat and vest. Then he took off his shirt and pants and put on a bathrobe. He had no manner or self-respect.

I looked at him with distaste and disgust. "No, I'd say Lazarus owned the show. He *is* the show!"

"He just works for me," said Price, in a most sardonic manner.

I knew from the first second he opened his mouth that the act he put on for the public was just a sham. I was hoping he'd get a charley horse in his tongue. Everything about him was repulsive and irritating, and my high opinion of barkers suddenly dropped. He was the first man I knew who blew his own horn and sounded taps at the same time. Immediately, in my own mind, I formed the Anti-Charlie Price Society. "I would like to speak with Mr. Lazarus, if I could," I said.

Again, Charlie Loudmouth took over. "Ya see why I handle the publicity. Ya just called him *Mr.* Lazarus. He is The Great Lazarus! I'll answer all the questions ya want ta know."

I knew there was only one way to stop this blowhard, and that was to hit him with a subject—I was now sure—he seldom brought up in front of Lazarus. "Well," I said, "you must be a very wealthy man."

"Whacha mean?" he asked, not sure he wanted to answer the question.

"Well, at fifty cents admission and three hundred people in the audience, that's about one hundred and seventy-five dollars a show. You do four performances a day, that's about $3500 a week."

"Yeah, but I got lot of expenses," he said defiantly.

"You mean like this lovely dressing room?" I said, looking around. "What's wrong with it? All he uses it for is to change clothes."

"He lives here ten hours a day," I said, "and $3500 a week is a lot of money even if you say it fast. But, then, I guess Lazarus receives most of the money."

"No," said Lazarus, "I get five hundred a week."

"Yeah," I said, folding my tablet so that Mr. Price would think I was going to leave, "five hundred a week for an attraction like Lazarus, that's *big* money, especially when you consider that an act like this is being presented in every theater in the country." I turned to Lazarus. "I'll tell you what. If you ever want to leave this outfit, I'll pay you two thousand dollars a week."

Mr. Price was angry and wanted to get off the subject. In fact, what he really wanted to do was get rid of me.

"I thought ya wanted ta know about Lazarus. Ya said it was an interview, not a financial report!"

"It will be an interview if I can speak with Mr. Lazarus!"

Price gave me a cold, comprehensive surveillance from head to foot. "Two thousand a week!" He leaned toward Lazarus. "Go with a guy like this, he'd steal ya blind." Then he turned back to me and, if looks could kill, he'd be a mass murderer.

He destroyed all the charm I once pictured a barker having. Everything unbecoming to a human being, *he* represented. His faced sagged and his eyes became beady. His forehead wrinkled into a frown. From the stare that Lazarus gave him, I was certain that Price had become insignificant in Lazarus' mind, unless he had become the enemy. But Lazarus stayed the gentleman and didn't lose his majestic deportment. I then realized that what he was doing on stage had a message; he transcended gross and material limitations.

"Sit down, Charlie. Have a glass of lemonade and cool off," said Lazarus.

The real tension was broken when the nurse returned with the hot dogs. She was all smiles as her well-shaped body glided into the tent. "I didn't know if you wanted chile, mustard, pickles, or onions, so brought a little of each. You can put it on yourself."

"Put it on myself?" said Lazarus. "Wouldn't it taste better on the hot dog?"

We all laughed, except the brooding swindler.

17

Lazarus asked, "You want a hot dog? They are good. Boy, I could eat a whole litter of these things. You know, they have great food value in them."

The nurse said, "They are good, but you have to know the brand. I got one the other day that had a feather in it."

Lazarus laughed. "It must have been a bird dog!"

"Ya got another show ta do," said Price. "Ya better get some rest." He turned to me and his look was infernal. "What he does on stage takes a lot out of 'em." he said, giving Lazarus a pat on the shoulder.

"Yeah," I said, "dying ain't easy!" I paused. "I hate to lose you with my reminiscences, but $3500 a week, and only an output of about $500?"

"Don't forget the income tax!" shouted Mr. Price.

"I file them," I retorted.

Lazarus only smiled. He seemed to realize I was egging Price on, and gave me a wink.

"Well," I said as I slapped my knee and sat back in my most uncomfortable chair, "I'd like to ask about your reaction to this little epic."

"If you are referring to money," said Lazarus, "That has never been the object with me."

"What is your object? Better yet, let me ask that question of Mr. Price. I know you are not a connoisseur with highly refined tastes, but how do you classify this exhibit?"

He answered quickly. "It's show business, entertainment, and oddity."

"Don't you think $3500 a week is more than an oddity?" I winked at Lazarus and continued, "And *you* are the star." I turned back to Price. "Don't you think the star is worth half of what is coming in?"

"Well," said Price, muddling and stammering, "I have expenses. The roustabouts, the doctors are fifty bucks a show, plus the nurses, and the privileges I pay to travel with the carnival. Then there's the publicity, hotels, travel expenses, and his comforts."

I waved my hand around the tent. "This is comfort?" I quickly apologized. "I am sorry, that was a low blow. I don't understand your way of life." I shook my head, trying to shake off the remark, but I made it for a reason. I just wanted to prod this thief. I just couldn't understand why Lazarus didn't ask more money for his services. He wasn't a novelty act, but a phenomenon.

When I asked him if it didn't concern him that Price was making a fortune off his talent, Lazarus said, "I receive five hundred dollars a week. That's not bad, considering that most people die for nothing."

"But you are not something seen everyday. There is a mystery about you, a stigmata, a resemblance to the crucifixion."

Lazarus sipped his lemonade, then said most innocently, "He didn't get paid either." Then he became philosophical. "This is my period of existence, so I do not have any feeling about the wicked who are prospering about me. I commune with my heart. You see, the world is a deceiver, yet each thing serves a purpose. Things happen for us to detect, but in the midst of this world of pleasure and its pursuit, the detection is impossible. Even *I* search for pleasure but I am different from most others. I paint, I write, I compose music. I fill my soul by creating. I am also learning something: those in pursuit have nothing but a delusion of adequacy."

"Tell me, is there some gimmick to your performance?"

"There must be, but what it is, I don't know. But let me correct you on one phrase. You used the word 'performance.' I am not a performer. Freak of nature, maybe, but I am not a mystic, not a magician, not a singer or dancer. I am, I believe, a subject for medical science to investigate. If there were some gimmick that could be exposed, I would be the first to have it known. But then, I think it's best to be kept a secret because children could become interested and that could cause a problem. You know they have a persistent curiosity. But to live, I die. If I were to expose any secret that I do have, I would truly die from guilt."

19

"He's got his secrets I don't even ask about," said Price.

For the first time since meeting him, I saw another side of Lazarus. He shouted at Price, "You don't know anything about what I do, only *I* know." He immediately became apologetic. "It's nothing I am ashamed of, but wouldn't it be dangerous for me to be exposed?" He stood up and seemed to retreat into another world for a moment. "Do you know how many people would try to do what I do, for religious purposes? My God, do you know what life after death would really do to religion, if everyone could die and return? The one great mystery of life would be solved. The church would die; there would be no reason for belief or good. All I know is that there is no self-hypnosis involved in what I do. There is nothing but willpower. That is the only explanation I can put into the minds of the innocents."

"Do you feel you are proof of life after death?" I asked.

"I've never given that any thought." He pondered for a moment and then shook his head. "You know, he continued, "if I am proof of life after death, there would be no goodness. There would be no law or fear of punishment. You see, I believe that religion is no more than faith and is accepted only by belief."

"Are you an atheist?" I asked.

"Not at all. I believe that man was made in the image of God. I believe in self, so I must believe in God. He is part of me, a part of all living things. There is a great natural force, it's the nature of all things. I believe in the welfare of others. I believe that a lot of people misunderstand a lot of things in the Bible. For instance, 'The weak shall inherit the earth.' I think that means if you are lazy and don't earn your way, and if you are weak and don't show ambition, you *are* going to inherit the earth. About six feet of it. No more, for if you let your spirit die, you'll soon be buried with it.

"As for being an atheist, there is really no such thing. Everyone, even the atheist believes in something. He just isn't sure there's a God. Yet, he talks more about God than the most devout monk. And how silly to believe there is no God! If something does not exist, it is nothing. So to get about preaching about nothing makes the atheist as nutty as a grove of walnut trees. Without church or religion, without fear of death or its social surpression, evil could not be solved or destroyed. Certainly, I can't solve many of my own problems. I can't answer anything about life after death. I don't have any desire to teach or make suggestions for others. When I see people in a crowd, they are not people, just bodies and faces, some friendly, but most of them potential enemies. I have no desire to change them."

Then I ask, "Do you have any escapes, such as, well, do you drink?"

"I have no need to drink," he replied. "I see things as reflections. Like a diamond, everything sparkles. Let's just say that I am not a biblical scholar," he concluded, taking a bit of his hot dog.

"Are you married?"

"No," he said with an innocent wave of his hand.

"But you have a family?"

"My mother died when I was born. My father, who knows!"

"Did anyone tell you about your mother?"

"I saw my mother in a photograph. She was a beautiful lady, I was told. She had long red hair, blue eyes, and she was tall and stately."

"You have the photograph with you?"

"No. There was only one photograph. It hung over my crib. When I was a year old, the house we lived in burned to ashes, and the photograph was destroyed."

"You remember the photograph? Amazing!"

"Yes. In fact, I see her each time I die on stage."

"Could you tell me just what happens when you go into your spell, or whatever you call it? Do you feel that you go over the brink?"

He smiled. "If I did, I wouldn't be here now. I will say that should I lose my willpower I could step over that brink. It would be similar to those who take drugs. One pill makes them forget a little, so why not go farther? So they take more until they are addicted, and desire even a greater escape. They step over the brink because they lack willpower. I have no desire for self-destruction."

"Do you think what you do helps mankind to understand life?"

"We only understand what we want to understand. In truth, we are all phonies! Take a girl with a beautiful body. She hides it with clothing. In the eyes of some, she is proper and beautiful. Should she expose her beauty, she becomes vulgar. If someone is intelligent and shows his intelligence, he is a show-off. If he hides it, he is called stupid. So you see, it is difficult to make people understand, but even more difficult to understand people. If you are right, someone will prove you wrong. You can't win for losing. It reminds me of the little girl who was thrown out of a parochial school for swearing, and then was kicked out of public school for praying."

"Could you give me some idea of what it's like, this spiritual trip you take? You said you see your mother each time you die. Could you explain that more?"

He didn't answer.

After several moments of silence I continued. "If you don't feel it's of concern to anyone, I'll understand. I do have respect for your personal thoughts and privacy, and I'm not here to belittle, only to report the truth. How do you feel as you fade away, and what keeps that willpower?"

"Ah, as I said before, that is the answer—willpower." He thought for a moment and then spoke as if he were repeating some words given to him by a voice only he could hear. His voice sounded different and his words seemed to me—saintly. "You asked about seeing my mother. Each time it's like a dream. It's difficult to explain, but each time I return to feel blessed and completely exhausted. At first I feel myself surrounded by many thoughts. They are like flashes. Sometimes, for instance, I see an aquaintance with the lovely face of a stranger. Quickly, I see her problems and, in a split second, I have solved them. Within another second I enter into a Shangrila of beauty. Ugliness is beyond my reach. I see myself smile and wave it away. I hear the voices of those around me, but they are muffled. I look for something to hate, to condemn, but I find no faults. Then I hear the doctor on stage say, 'He is dead.' At that moment I feel myself reaching back to where I have traveled from. I turn back, then I hear the words, 'I shall feel no evil.' I hear sounds like pea gravel being poured on a galvanized chute. I see objects that look like blue smoke from an extinguished candle, swelling into space. There is the fragrance of flowers, possibly the perfume worn by the attending nurse. Then I feel like I am speeding through a tunnel so fast that I find it hard to breathe. Then there is a light in the distance, the size of a pinhole. I feel as if I am a spigot and the faucet has been turned on. There is a rattling vibration like an earthquake—everything shakes but my body. I feel as if I am traveling through water at a high speed. The pinhole becomes larger. Suddenly, there is the powder blue brightness of the sun and space. I feel a hand and see this lady over my crib. She guides me through the tunnel as everything races to the entrance. It is a vast emptiness, a nothingness. Again I smell fragrant flowers. It *is* the perfume the nurse is wearing. I know I am returning as the vibration feels as if it is breaking every bone in my body. It is a near-death encounter; I almost reach enlightenment. Though, if I ever have I can't remember it, even though, at times, when I return I can correctly answer questions on subjects I know nothing about." He paused and took a sip of lemonade.

It was an impressive performance he had just given. His voice and the way he pictured each move made it seem as if he had been holding all of this inside him and had never really been able to express his feelings before. I looked toward him. It was like seeing a face in the clouds. I had to blink to shake the image. I almost had the same feeling I had when I dreamed I was flying. It seemed so real that when I awoke I tried to fly. This connection helped me understand Lazarus' feeling. I wondered if, perhaps, we are all close to death when we sleep. I wondered if there were some way that those really interested in life could submit themselves to a test that would monitor deep sleep? I began to wonder if sleep could actually be a prologue of death? Is it a sort of an introduction to the end? I then asked Lazarus, "Would you say that what you experience is something beyond a deep sleep or nightmarish dream?"

I couldn't answer that," he said in a most gentle tone, "for I haven't dreamed your dream. I am not a person who analyzes dreams, nor am I a student of witchcraft or the powers of the imagination. I live life and don't wish to lose it until I live its full potentialty."

He thought for a second. "We are all here for a purpose. I don't know enough about life to investigate death any closer."

"How do you feel when you return?"

He didn't respond with set answers, as if he had heard all those questions before. "Sometimes," he said, "I have a tremendous headache, other times I am famished. I guess it's the closest thing to birth, for I have a desire for strange combinations of food, much like pregnant women who ask for ice cream and pickles, or white asparagus. Sometimes I must have a large steak with raw onions, and milk. I always have a craving for milk."

Mr. Price broke the lovely spell. "That's another expense—steaks and milk!"

"Yes," I said, "I can understand, at twenty-five cents a pound it sure cuts into that $3500 a week."

"Are ya trying to make him believe I'm a crook!" shouted Price.

"I couldn't change my own thinking, no matter what you are."

Price became beligerent. "O.K., Buddy, I think ya got enough, in fact too much, too much for a small town paper. No matter what ya print, I'll sue ya for slander."

24

"Come on, Charlie, lay off the man. There is no need for the way you are acting," suggested Lazarus. Then he turned back to me. "Is there anything else I can help you with?"

"Is Lazarus your given name?"

"Yes," he said with pride. "Ishmael Joseph Lazarus. Three biblical names."

"Tell me, are you a psychic? Can you predict the future?"

"No, but my father was psychic. He knew the day, the hour, and the minute he was going to die."

"Really! How does one know those things?"

"Well, the sheriff told my father!" Lazarus smiled. We all laughed.

"On the way over here I saw lots of graffiti sprayed on the rocks. One sign in particular said, 'God is dead.' What's your thought on that?"

"I think whoever wrote that should erase it. God is not dead. I talk to him before each performance."

"One more question. It's said, 'When one goes beyond a point, the brain dies.' How do you explain that? I mean I find you quite intelligent even after you've been officially proclaimed dead so many times."

"I am able, by some supernatural strength, to keep the flow of oxygen in my blood stream, that air needed to support my life. Or, maybe my brain is enriched with oxygen before I go under. If I am oxygenated it is something a brain specialist would have to diagnose or explain in medical terms."

I am amazed how he answered questions without hesitation. I looked at the nurse, who was wiping her eyes with a handkerchief. She seemed touched not by what he said, but by the sincerity with which he said it. I glanced at Price and I couldn't help noticing the same devious expression he had before. I made up my mind to always dislike him. I will teach my children to dislike him. By the time I have grandchildren, hating Mr. Price will be a family tradition.

Lazarus stood up. "Well, that's about all the time I can give you, but I want to thank you. You've given me a chance to vent my consciousness, you have lifted that invisible screen and made it visible."

As I started to leave, Mr. Price, trying to be apologetic, stammered, "Thanks for stopping in. Ya want a ticket for the next show?"

"No, I have to try and write a story." I turned to Lazarus, shook his hand, and asked, "Do you think you will know when you are not coming back?"

"Only you will know, I won't. A question for you. Do you know if you will get home alive?"

"If I don't," I said with a chuckle, "only you will know! Well, I think I have enough for a story."

He took my hand and I felt that strange warmth again. "Just be careful what you write," he said, "There are a lot of thrill seekers. Someone could take one misleading statement and take a step toward death." As we walked to the tent's entrance, he continued, "I hope I haven't said anything that would misguide someone into an experiment they know nothing about. The safer way to explain my feeling is to say that it is the same as it is when you are very tired and lay down and doze off. When you wake up, you say, 'I must have dozed off.' You don't remember falling into sleep."

I thought for a second. "Would you say that death and sleep are kindred souls?"

"No," he replied, "with sleep you wake up. But I would say it's as close as you're going to get. I do believe we should all say, long before we go to sleep, 'The Lord is my Shepherd.' Then you will rest, for you will dream. As long as you dream you are alive. You may not remember your dream, but you will remember you are alive."

I shook his hand. On the way out I said to Price, "I am sorry for any misunderstanding." Then I looked toward Lazarus. "In case you want a new job, my offer still stands. "I'll pay you two thousand a week."

The nurse winked and said, as she extended her hand, "It was nice meeting you. I hope we will meet again."

"I'd give you a call but I don't know your number."

"It's in the phone book," she said with a smile.

"I don't know your name."

"It's in the book, too. Right next to my husband's name."

"What do they call him?"

"Jealous," said the nurse.

Again we all laughed, and I left.

•   •   •

The next day I want back to make closer observations of Lazarus' performance, but when I arrived at the carnival lot, his tent had been taken down and I couldn't find him. It almost seemed I had dreamed something that had never happened.

On the way back to the office I went into the Lunch Wagon, a popular diner which was always packed. I was seated at a table, alone, when I looked up and there was the nurse, standing in line waiting to be seated. She was with a big fellow who was dressed in anything but the latest fashion. In fact, I couldn't help wondering how a guy like that could get such a beautiful girl. I got up and told the waitress I'd be right back. I walked up to the nurse. She was wearing a coat over her uniform because it had suddenly turned cold overnight.

"Hello, I said, "I'm Jim Lawson from the newspaper."

"Oh, yes, how are you? This is my husband, Harold Fenmore."

I invited them to sit at my table. The place was so crowded there would be a long wait, so they accepted. After their orders were taken, I asked, "Tell me what happened to The Great Lazarus."

"Oh boy, it was knock down and drag out after you left."

"A fight?"

"Only with words. Mr. Lazarus was too much of a gentleman for a fight."

"What happened?"

"Well, at first, I didn't pay much attention. Mr. Price said

27

to Lazarus, 'That reporter,' (meaning you), 'has given me a hell of an idea. We're going ta sell religion!'

"Lazarus said, 'I want to talk about my salary.' Price told him they would after he told him about his idea. Lazarus just sat slumped down in his chair. He turned to me and asked for a glass of lemonade. I got it for him. 'That creep,' Price said, 'that's another expense. Them lemons don't grow on trees!" Then he pulled his chair up real close to Lazarus. He tried to act nice, but he still had that sardonic attitude about him. He said to Lazarus, 'What's the biggest money making racket you can think of?'

"Lazarus said, 'The IRS.'

" 'No,' said Price, religion! We are going to start a religious organization." Lazarus told him he wasn't interested in religion, he was interested in discussing his salary. Price got angry and told him to forget the salary talk, they were going to make more money than Lazarus ever heard of. Then he started to make his pitch again.

"You know," she interjected, "that guy is bad from his grammar to his smile to his attitude to his manners. Well, he lays all this stuff on Lazarus about going to a school where they teach religion. Lazarus told him, 'You'd better go to public school before you try a school of theology.' Price told him he'd become an evangelist, get ordained, grow a beard, wear a white robe, and preach the book. He figured he'd need a big tent that would hold at least a thousand. About the second night of each crusade, Lazarus would pull his death act, then Price would bring him back. Then they would pass the plate and, wham, they'd be rich in no time.

"Then Mr. Lazarus asked, 'What miracle would you perform the next night?' Price said he'd hire some crippled, blind, and deaf jokers that he would cure. Of course, they'd all be shills.

"Lazarus said, "Why don't you go into towns where it's cold and they have no electricity and sell wood-burning blankets? It has about as much logic.' Then Lazarus got very angry. In fact, the way he changed really frightened me. I never thought it was in him. He took Price by his lapels and said, 'You sanctimonious hypocrite, you must be the only living brain donor in the world. What are you going to do in the next town? I can see the headlines: EVANGELIST BRINGS MAN BACK TO LIFE THE SECOND TIME!'

"Price said, 'Well, yer doin' it four times a day now.' But Lazarus reminded him that he wasn't selling religion now. He pointed to heaven and said, 'I have a feeling that whoever is up there wouldn't be too happy about making death a money-making religious mockery.' Price told him that they would only play places 'where God don't go.'" She shook her head. "Boy, is that man dumb!

"Lazarus told him he wanted to talk about his salary. 'What the hell do you think you are worth?' Price asked. Lazarus looked him right in the eye and said, 'About two thousand a week.'"

"I guess I got to Lazarus," I said.

"You sure did. And Price really got mad. He yelled, 'You were nothin' when I found ya! Ya pull this on me and I'll blackball ya in show business, you'll never work again.'

"I thought Lazarus was going to punch him. He said, 'Look, you idiot, if you try that religious stunt, you know what will happen? You'll have people digging up dead relatives by the hundreds, and when you don't bring them back to life, you know what happens? You are going to be head man at the first religious lynching! Now, I'm going to the hotel.' He put on his white suit. 'Meanwhile, think about my salary.'"

The nurse's husband interrupted. "You were in the tent with a guy dressing?"

"My back was turned," she said. Then, she continued with the story. "He put on a white Panama hat. Price looked at it and asked, 'Where did you get the new Panama hat?' And, then, as if nothing had happened, Price says, 'You know, when I was younger I was stationed in Panama.'"

She started laughing. "Lazarus said, 'I guess that's why they put locks on the Canal Zone.' Then he walked out, saying, 'I'll be at my hotel when you make up your mind.'

"Well, evidently, Price didn't give him the salary. I went to work the next day and everything was moved out."

And that was the last I heard of The Great Lazarus for a few years.

CHAPTER THREE

It was by accident I met him, again. I was at a new's convention. We talked at length, and from that moment on he kept in touch with me. I gave him my address and phone number. I couldn't prove the things he did, but everytime I heard about a robbery I put one and one together.

With the help of his idiopathic powers, Lazarus became, perhaps, the greatest con artist who ever walked down a crooked path. With him it was a science. Everything he did was systematically arranged with a great knowledge of the physical and natural world. With each new disguise he became a new person. He was very precise about each detail and made sure that he didn't fall back into the habits or mannerisms of the last person he had been. The one constant was his kindness, and that he never took advantage of anyone who earned an honest dollar.

But he really had no identity. His social security number was forged; he would change numbers with each identity. He always managed to keep out of camera range, so there were no photographic records, just mock-up sketches. And he changed his appearance after each job; it was like being robbed by a dead man. He had no fingerprints on file, even though he had once come close. It was after that escapade that I developed a sort of gruesome attachment to him. I admired his class and his guts.

As I said, he was almost fingerprinted. It happened down South, in a small town that was notorious for its speed trap. The local police were a real bunch of rednecks. Lazarus was passing through on a Greyhound bus and this particular town was a one hour rest stop, so Lazarus got off the bus to stretch his legs. He was wandering around, sightseeing in the drab village. Before returning to the bus he went into a gas station restroom. When he came out, two cops grabbed him and started pushing him around. They made him put his hands on top of the squad car and spread his legs. One officer frisked his body, handcuffed him and threw him into the back seat of the squad car. Then they took him to the police station, about a block from the bus stop.

While going through the door of the station entrance, one of the officers poked him in the ribs to hurry him along. "What the hell was that for?" Lazarus asked.

"Nothing," said the officer, giving him a shove. Then he leaned so close Lazarus could inhale his breath, and he said, "So you can imagine what you'll get if you try something."

They entered a small, smelly room. At the far end of the cubical, seated at a desk that looked like a busted Hefty Bag, with a mess of papers and a small nameplate that said, "Chief J. Stanton," sat a big, fat, sloppy man. Based on his poundage, a weight chart would indicate that he should be eight feet tall. If he were to go into a restaurant alone, the waitress would ask if he wanted separate checks. His fat jaws gave him pig eyes. He looked like a "Beware of Vicious Dog" sign. There he sat, shirt collar open, with all three chins resting on his chest. Had it been Halloween, he would have looked normal. He sat like mute, loose blubber in an overstuffed swivel chair behind his desk. After several minutes of "let 'em wait," he looked up. "Well, what do we have here?" he demanded, throwing his pencil on the papers before him.

The arresting officer, as if asking for approval, read the report. "We caught this *Yankee* boy prowling around the gas station," he said as he removed the handcuffs from Lazarus' wrists.

They fingerprinted him and booked him on suspicion of

robbery, assaulting an officer, resisting arrest, disturbing the peace, and loitering. Then, they fined him $500, all before Lazarus could say a word.

"Just put your belongings on the desk," commanded the chief. When the wallet was placed on the desk, he opened it and took out the $500 fine. Saying, "Let justice prevail," and folding the money, he continued, "Now what was you doin' walkin' around town?"

Lazarus shrugged his shoulders. "Just walking. I wasn't *doing* anything."

"Well, Sir, when folks don't have anything to do, they don't do it around here."

Lazarus noticed a young lady sitting nearby. She was dabbing her tearful eyes with her handerchief. Apparently, she had been arrested for a traffic misdemeanor. Lazarus looked back at the chief. "Now that I see I have a witness," he said, referring to the lady, with a nod of his head, "may I make my one phone call? It's my constitutional right."

"Oh," exclaimed the chief, sarcastically, "now we don't wanna break the Constitution!" He pointed with a nod of his head. "There's a pay phone right over there."

Lazarus took a coin from his belongings on the desk, walked to the phone, and dialed a number. "Yes, operator," he said, as he backed away from the phone to see the number. "This number is 595-5000, and reverse the charges. It's an emergency."

Mockingly, the chief parroted, "This is an emergency." He laughed. "He don't know the half of it."

Now, what the chief didn't know was that the friend on the other line was me. I knew Lazarus was in trouble as soon as I heard his phoney conversation, so I just let him do all the talking. He spoke loudly. "Hello! This is Harold Snodgrass." Then he changed his tone. "Oh, hello dear."

Again, the chief mocked Lazarus. "Hello, dear!"

"Will you put Governor Green on, please."

The chief changed his smart attitude and became more interested.

"Hello, Governor Green. Yes, I am in Pottville. And I've been arrested, pushed around, and harrassed." He paused. "It's pretty bad, sir, even worse. The corruption here is unbelievable."

The tall officer grabbed the phone from Lazarus. "Hello, who is this?" he shouted into the phone.

In a stern voice, I said, "This is Governor Green. *Who am I talking to?*"

"This is Officer Morris."

I was enjoying the play acting and tried to become even more convincing. "Well, Officer Morris, you tell Snodgrass I am sending federal agents *right down there.* You also tell him to get back on the case he is assigned to."

The confused officer held the phone toward the chief, as if to say, you had better handle this. After a struggle to get out of his chair, the chief waddled to the phone, like a elephant looking for a mate. The officer handed the phone to the anxious chief. "It's the Governor," said the officer, covering the mouthpiece, "and he is mad as hell!"

The chief tried to speak with a gentle, friendly authority. "Hello, Governor Green. There has been a little mix-up down here, but it is all straightened out now. Yes sir, I'll tell him. Nice talking to you. You probably don't remember me—Chief Stanton. I was one of the officers who drove you around down here during the last election." He pulled the phone away from his ear and looked in the receiver as if he had been hit by a stungun. Lazarus knew that I had slammed down the receiver on its cradle at the other end. The chief, like a deflated blimp, wobbled back to his desk and pointed to Lazarus' belongings. "You're free to go. I didn't know!"

"Well, you do now," Lazarus replied angrily.

"Sorry about the delay," said the mumbling chief.

Lazarus suddenly increased his aggravation and irritation. "If that guy gets away, you are going to really be sorry. I can't believe this. You talk about misconduct of an officer!" He then looked at the tall officer and shook his head.

"Gee whiz!" the officer said in disbelief.

"Here, take your things and hurry. Don't want you to miss that bus," said the chief as he wiped sweat from his pudgy face.

'I'll take these fingerprints, too," Lazarus said, grabbing the card, looking at it as if he had been disgraced, and then putting it in his pocket.

"Help yourself, by all means." The chief was being very cooperative.

Lazarus started to leave, but turned back. "Oh, and don't forget my $500."

"Ahmmm, I do hope you overlook this incident," said the chief. "I am sorry it happened, but you know how these rookies are!"

"Yes, I do! Tell me, how long have you been a rookie?"

The chief forced a chuckle. "That one's on me." He then addressed the officer who was observing all of this in utter dismay. "You just remember, there is always someone higher up with a little more authority than you."

Lazarus turned to the sobbing lady. "What do they have you charged with, Miss?"

"A minor traffic violation. But the things they said to me were humiliating."

Lazarus turned back to the chief. "You know, it is Mr. Big's like you who make the world overcrowded." Pointing to a purse on the desk, he asked the lady, "Is this your purse?"

"Yes, sir."

He handed the purse to her. "Do you live around here?"

"No, I was just passing through. I'm on my way to Lawrenceburg. My little girl is in the hospital there and I was hurrying to see her."

Lazarus turned and looked at the chief. "You know what? You are *nothing* else," he said in disgust.

The chief became belligerent. "Now just one minute!" he

bellowed as he struggled to get out of the tight-fitting chair. "Just who in the hell do you think you is?"

"I *is* Harold Snodgrass, Special Investigator for the FBI. That's who I is."

"I didn't see any I.D. with that information."

"If you had, I wouldn't be a *special* investigator!" said Lazarus, using a thick, mocking southern accent. "Do you think you would have let me call the governor if you had seen that information? Do you?" Then Lazarus calmed down. "Look, you are in enough trouble, and you are going to have a lot of explaining to do when those federal agents get here. They'll want to know about obstruction of justice, abusive language, misconduct of a police officer, etc., etc."

"He's right, Chief, don't make it worse," pleaded Officer Morris.

"Ah, shut your mouth!" shouted the chief. "This is all your messing up, you got me into . . ."

Lazarus got his wallet and put it into his pocket as he interrupted the chief's tirade. "Now I've got a bus to catch."

"Yeah," said the nervous chief, "you don't want to miss your bus."

"I'll see you in federal court!" said Lazarus as he took the lady by the arm. "Come on, Mam, let's get out of the graft pit." They both hurried out of the police station.

"I am grateful to you," she said.

They reached her car and Lazarus, in a stage whisper, said, "Just get the hell out of town."

"Can I drive you to the bus?"

"Good idea."

She drove the car a block to the bus, parked in front of it, and prevented it from leaving until Lazarus could get on.

"Goodbye," Lazarus shouted as he got out of the car and ran to the door of the bus.

"I sure do thank you," shouted the lady.

The bus driver opened the door, Lazarus got on, and the bus was on its way.

36

CHAPTER FOUR

In my later years, I often wondered what had happened to all the colorful, great people with their strange, yet special, talents who entertained the public. But the one name that constantly came to mind was The Great Lazarus. He was ghost-like in my memory—not the sort of disembodied spirits of the dead that are imagined to be wandering about and haunting the living. Perhaps that, but with a difference: he was, in truth, a ghost-like mystery with a human skin.

I couldn't think of him without remembering his extraordinary skill or, maybe I should say, tricks. What I would give to know his secret, to know how he outsmarted the one thing in life that has kept men in bondage—the fear of death. He did not fear it. What was his mysterious formula? What was the power that made him able to perform the spellbinding feat? With today's modern electronics and computer monitors I wonder if he would have been able to avoid being branded a fraud? I am certain they would have been able to detect self-hypnosis or some other hoodwinking gimmick.

Anyway, when he disappeared I put everything aside and went on a search for him, for what better story could there be? But I not only wanted to do a story, I also wanted to do research; I would offer him enough money to devulge his secret.

Well, what I discovered was a story so strange . . . but, then, the truth is so real that it borders on fiction. If that is so, who cares, as long as the character is colorful and entertaining. And Lazarus was certainly both.

But first, let's go back and take a quick look at the entertainment that helped build our society before the drastic changes that have all but wiped out show business. Gone are the great schools for actors and comedians, such as the medicine shows, those sandlot stages where they gave free entertainment, then sold their product. They call it television now. Gone are the tent shows and the minstrel shows that were murdered by local lodges and fraternities that presented local minstrel shows so often that even the smallest town was saturated with black face comedians and barbershop quartets. The local productions killed the novelty and charm of the large traveling minstrel shows that included such performers as Docsteader, Neil O'Brien, Al G. Fields, Lasses White, Sugar Foot Gaffiney, and Bert Swore, all of whom were eventually reduced to insignificance. Then went burlesque, a real family entertainment that, even at its worst, couldn't use subject matter now seen regularly on TV and in concert halls. But at this time it was considered family entertainment. The circus disappeared because of the city permits which halted the 11:45 and the parade down Main Street, and because the railroad expenses and the union demands finally made the costs prohibitive. Then came the motion picture which wounded vaudeville and New York stage productions. When talking pictures were introduced, live stage shows and vaudeville were doomed.

Anyhow, after a several months of traipsing around booking agent offices and reading the theatrical tabloids, such as *Variety* and *Billboard,* I discovered that The Great Lazarus was around, but he was ham and egging it, playing tank towns. There were even jokes about him. "Vaudeville is dead and Lazarus is asking it to move over," and "He is the only act that dies and gets paid for it," or, "If my act dies, I get canceled, Lazarus gets applause."

He was playing towns that didn't, as yet, have talking pictures, so the audience was still there for stage shows. But his bookings were few and far between. Some theater managers wouldn't book him because they felt that the audience wanted to leave the theater happy, not to come out saying that the act was gruesome. This reduced Lazarus to renting an empty store front on a side street, building a platform, and charging fifty cents to play before a meager audience. Business was so bad that if someone called and asked when the show started, the reply would be, "When can you be here?"

He obviously didn't enjoy the life of a gypsy because I learned he was also working in secret. He had turned the act into a new profession as a jewel robber.

Apparently, along about this time, Lazarus married an elderly lady who was killed when the motorcycle she was riding hit a wet spot in the road and she was hurled some fifty feet into the river. Some wags said that he tried to rescue her by throwing her a rubber tire. Unfortunately, he left the rim in it. But she must have loved him, for she willed him her full estate. (Remember, that would have been before inheritance taxes.) He sold the farm for about sixty thousand dollars, only to learn a year later that they had discovered oil on the land. But he invested his sale money and earned enough to enter the social set.

He was always seen in the company of beautiful ladies, but he never remarried, figuring, I guess, that at some point a wife wants to know everything about your past, and he was certain she would ask him to give her his secret. If he didn't, the wife would give him the Noxema face cream treatment and cut off the bedroom capers.

Now and then, he would rehearse his dying act to keep in shape because he worried that he would forget how to die.

One day I picked up a newspaper and read about a robbery that could only be connected to Lazarus.

From what I was able to learn, he began his new profession in St. Louis when he was invited to a party given by a Mrs. Lillian Kent, wife of a local beer baron, for a friend of her's whose husband (a man much older than she) died and left her with millions of dollars. The friend's name was Lisa Kinmore, a woman about forty-five, without a wrinkle or a sign of stress, although she had been widowed only three months. She was very attractive so she hadn't reached that stage where her make-up cracked after three hours. Her long blond hair looked as if an invisible hairdresser was constantly at her side to keep each hair in place. The software she toted on her fingers, neck, and arm added up to a fortune. She sparkled so much she looked like she was plugged in.

Normally, she was the life of the party, but not lately, for she and her husband had been deeply devoted to each other. Now, however, she was sedate and dignified. That is, until Lazarus walked into the Kent's beautiful home, which was old, but it had been opulently and tastefully refurbished on the inside. Lazarus scanned the guests as he entered until Lisa's loveliness came into his wandering gaze.

Mrs. Kent took him by the arm and walked him toward Lisa. "Come," she said, "I want you to meet a dear friend, who is a widow. I think you can cheer her up." She escorted Lazarus to where Lisa was seated. The second her sight fell upon him, a strange sensation surged through her body. In fact, she even blushed. She had a flashback to her first high school date. Mrs. Kent was giggling like a matchmaker. "Lisa, I want you to meet Larry King."

Lazarus had changed his name. In fact, he had done so several times during the past few years. He gave a slight bow as she extended her hand to him. The moment she touched his hand her whole body seemed to vibrate. I could understand this since I remember the first time I shook his hand. Such a touch! She must have noticed the same sensation because she held his hand longer than a lady normally would at a first meeting. She was completely taken by his gentleness.

Mrs. Kent was pleased to see Lisa had livened up and become her old self again. "Now, I want you to get to know each other," she said, giving Lisa's hand a little pat. "You'll find Mr. King a most interesting man."

Lisa realized that she was still holding his hand. "Oh!" she said, most embarrassed, "how rude of me."

"But it's quite enjoyable. And I'll cut it off and give it to you, if you want it," Lazarus said with a smile. They both chuckled as she reluctantly released her grip.

"Won't you sit down?" asked Lisa, as, with a royal gesture of her hand, she patted the cushion of the vacant chair next to her. "Strange, we haven't met before," she said.

"We have. But you wouldn't have noticed at such a distance? In theaters, restaurants, even once at the beach, I have seen you, but you didn't notice me."

Lisa was impressed. "Tell me, have you been friends with the Kent's long?"

"We are not old family acquaintances," he said as he seated himself.

"Business acquaintance?" she asked.

"I designed a new beer bottle for his company."

"A beer bottle?"

"Yes, the old one his brewery was using was too tall for modern refrigerators, so I cut the bottle down, and reshaped it. It contains the same amount of beer, but now the refrigerator will hold more bottles."

"So you are an inventor?"

"Not really. It just seemed like a more practical idea."

"What other ingenious ideas do you have?"

"Not ingenious, but ingenuous!"

"Ingenuous?"

"Yes," he said, smiling to take the edge off the concise 'ingenuous.' "It means 'little thoughts free from deceit.' And I disguise no thoughts." Lazarus leaned toward her. "It's good to see you smile."

"But life must go on," she said, with little belief in her statement.

"Yes, life is wonderful. I mean without it, you're dead"

"Yes," she said, "I just lost my husband."

"No, you didn't lose a husband, you gained a loving lasting memory."

She smiled, as if to say, "What a lovely thought."

He continued, "My grandmother was one hundred and two when she joined the heavenly choir. She was remarkable woman, with great wit. Her last words were, 'I never thought I'd live to see this day.'"

"You seem to be casual about life."

"No, I just don't believe you should worry about something that happens only occasionally. Me, I expect to live forever! It's good to see you out of your shell."

"It's nice, but I feel it's too soon after . . ."

"It's never too soon. Again, I speak of my grandmother. One week after her husband went to the great unemployment office in the sky, she put on a white dress and a big, wide-brim hat and went alone to the Saturday night dance. A couple of old bitties, you know the type, they have a wonderful sense of rumor! Well, this one lady said to my grandmother, 'My, you are all in white and out for a good time.' Granny said, 'Yep, time to kick up my heels.' The lady said, 'But your husband just died.' Granny replied, 'I know he died, but I didn't!' The old bitty said, 'What would your husband think?' Granny said, 'Well, if he's thinking, looks like we played a dirty trick on him because we buried him.' The old lady was shocked and said, 'Well, he's looking down on you right now.' Granny said, 'No. And you ladies better have on lots of petticoats because I knew him better than you did. And he isn't looking down, he's looking up!'"

"Didn't she feel bad at all?" asked Lisa as she laughed.

"Oh yes, but she would say, 'If worry and grieving could bring him back, I'd worry and grieve. He is giving me piece of mind, now that I know where he is at night.'"

Suddenly Lazarus noticed the gentleness in Lisa's eyes. For a second, he thought about giving her a demonstration and a lesson in how to cope with the grim reaper. It would be a perfect setting, he decided, as he looked around. There were a few doctors who, no doubt, would assist in the exhibition, but, then, they would take credit for their medical skill. Best to let those pill darlings of the hypochondriac set cool their hand on their cocktail glasses, as they talked about their golf and tennis games, or how much they earned in real estate. At best, he would wind up being the freak of the evening.

It was at that split second that a flash on Mrs. Kinmore's finger, brighter than the diamond on Harry Winston's Christmas tree, gave him a thought. "Why shouldn't I live in this splendor? Meet beautiful ladies, keep my dignity?" There was a better use for his talent; her jewelry fascinated him.

Suddenly, Lisa brought him out of his trance. "Are you all right?" she asked with warm concern.

"Yes, but for a second I seemed to hear an evil voice instructing me."

"I hope you don't feel it's because of me."

"No," he said, giving her a reassuring pat on the back of her hand. "You are too dear to provoke an evil thought." Her charm was overwhelming, but still he thought, "I want to relieve this dear lady of some of her burdens, something like ten pounds of diamonds, sapphires, and rubies. I'll just put those burdens in a small bag, just like jelly beans."

As he sat daydreaming, his expression was noticed by the other guests. They were pleased, especially for Lisa. They thought they were seeing a transfixed admiration—a man in a state of complete devotion. It was obvious that Lazarus did not realize he was staring so intently.

The spell was broken by Mrs. Kent. "You dear people," she said, flitting about, "seem so pleasant together that I have arranged the table seating so that you can get better acquainted." She stood with a hand on the shoulder of each. "How lovely."

Lazarus rose from his chair and extended his hand to help Lisa to her feet.

"Thank you kindly, sir," she said. Then, for a moment, she smiled in a musing manner. "It's been so long since I've received such courtious attention," she said, as she gave his hand a gentle squeeze. She took his arm like a giddy girl at her first prom, and they walked into the dining room.

His expression was a happy, triumphant smile. His eyes were fixed on hers and they didn't notice the other guests who were nudging each other, pointing out that it was the first time in some months they had seen Lisa so happy. One gentleman leaned toward Lisa. "It's good to see you among the living," he said in a most sincere tone.

"My," said Lisa, "has it been all that noticeable?"

Lisa sat at the head of the table, next to Lazarus and Mrs. Kent. Before dinner Mrs. Kent was almost in the same sort of trance as Lisa. Mr. Kent requested that all guests join hands, and then asked Lazarus to deliver a prayer. At first, Lazarus was a bit stunned, but he rose to the occasion.

His words were clear as his gentle voice echoed, "Dear God, we are grateful for what we have in this day's bountiful gift of loveliness, and for the warmth of friendship, for the understanding and meaning of life, we are grateful. We thank you for our incentive to be worthy of this second. Bless all faiths, bless all who keep those faiths. Amen."

There was silence as the napkins were placed on laps, and then the group returned to their conversations. I am sure that what he said was hosanna to all present and made them feel that he was a good man. But it was just another case of love in the voice and larceny in the heart.

Lazarus gave both ladies equal attention during the dinner. They found him to be charming and most witty, with his entertaining remarks on many subjects.

Lisa inquired, "Have you ever been married?"

"No, but there was one girl. I asked her why she wouldn't marry me, was there someone else? She replied, 'There *must* be!' He chuckled.

Lisa remarked, "You're the type who wears his heart on his sleeve."

Again, he chuckled, then said, "Well, that just goes to show, those transplants are not perfected."

"But I guess I am attentive. There was one girl who turned out to be a liar. She fibbed about everything. Not only did she lie about the size of her yacht, she made me do the rowing."

Mrs. Kent couldn't eat for laughing. She patted his arm after every remark. Then she said, "Has anyone ever told you how wonderful you are?"

Lazarus smiled and said, "They must have, it wasn't my idea!"

Lisa then wondered, "Have you asked any other girl to marry you?"

"Yes, but she didn't reply. I guess it's hard to talk when you laughing."

"Well, someday you'll ask a girl to change her name to yours," said Mrs. Kent in a prophetic tone.

Lazarus thought for a second. "I don't think so. Who would want a girl called Larry?"

After the enjoyable dinner, Lazarus and Lisa mingled with the other guests until it was time to say good night. Lisa asked Lazarus where he lived.

"A little beyond my means," he said. "I am at the Trymore Hotel."

"Can I drop you off at your hotel? One gets lonely driving, even if it's a Rolls Royce."

"Better than that. It is customary for the gentleman to see the lady to her door. Then I can take a cab from there."

Lisa was impressed with his gallantry.

"Lovely idea," said Mrs. Kent.

"I thank you," said Lazarus. "I have never ridden in a new Rolls Royce."

"Where is your home, Mr. King?" Mrs. Kent asked.

"San Francisco. I have a home there. It is a very old house. In fact, it is so old it is paid for."

Mr. Kent laughed and, turned to Lisa, said, "Isn't he awful? Mr. King, I hope you enjoy the ride in the Rolls."

"I don't know," said Lazarus, "if it is such a great car, why don't more people drive them?"

Lisa smiled. "Poverty."

"That I don't believe about poverty," he retorted. "One time

45

out in California I kept hearing about this so-called 'poverty,' so I made a survey on my own. I went to this little town, up one street, down the next. I knocked on every door and asked, 'Do you folks need anything? Is there poverty in your home?' Well, not only were they insulting to me, but also very abusive. I swore I would never go to Beverly Hills again!"

There were the usual front door conversations and good nights. (I've always thought it curious that folks go to a party all evening and not find anything worthwhile to talk about until they are supposed to go home.) The guests all got into their cars and left the Kent residence. About thirty minutes later, Lisa parked in front of the Kinmore Apartment building, a most impressive place with ferns, flowers, and shiny brass knobs on the beveled glass doors.

Lazarus opened the car door for Lisa and escorted her to the entrance. "I'll walk you to the elevator."

She hesitated, then asked, "Would you care to have a nightcap?"

He glanced at his watch. "It's rather late."

Lisa smiled and took his arm. "One drink won't make it too much later. I don't enjoy drinking at parties."

They walked though the lobby and entered the elevator. By the time they reached the top floor, Lazarus learned that she owned the building, that it was not community property, but given to her by her second husband, the late Mr. Kinmore. She was only staying in the penthouse overnight because she didn't want to drive the freeway at such a late hour.

When they reached the penthouse floor, Lazarus stepped into the alcove leading to a garden which was surrounded by a large wall. The entrance port was glassed in, but there was a clear view of the city.

Lisa stood in front of the door, searching through her purse. "How stupid of me. I forgot my keys." She turned to Lazarus and asked him to look under the statue, a small leprechaun. "There should be a spare key there."

He lifted the statue and found the key. He handed it to her. She opened the door and handed the key back to him.

"Would you put it back, in case I forget my key again."

They entered the hall. She turned on the light of the most expensively decorated room he had ever seen. She then opened the French door that led to the garden.

He stepped out and surveyed the view. "It's beautiful," he said.

She shrugged her shoulders and said, "Make yourself at home, I have to get out of these trinkets." She removed her earrings and necklace as she walked to the bedroom. He watched her in the wall mirror. She removed the jewelry and placed it in a gem box on top of the dresser. Then she removed her shoes and went into a dressing room. In a few minutes she came out wearing a lovely house coat of the latest fashion. Most women would have worn it for an evening dress. "Well," she said, "what will you have to drink?"

Lazarus tilted his head, as if to suggest that he didn't care. "I'm so tired, how about a little cup of hemlock or a poison asp?"

"How about a brandy?" she suggested.

"Fine?"

She left the room and, after a second, yelled, "It will only be a minute. I have to go to the liquor vault."

He listened for a second, then hurried to the hall and opened the front door. Then, he rushed into the bedroom, picked up the jewelry box, dashed to the garden and stashed the box in the bushes. Then he reached down, got some dirt and smeared it on his face. He reentered the room, knocked over a table and fell to the floor, where he messed his hair.

Lisa entered the room with a tray and two brandy glasses. As she set the tray on a table, she noticed him. "What happened?"

"Who was that?" asked Lazarus, pointing to the hall.

"Who was who? I didn't see anyone."

47

Lazarus got to his feet and moved to the hall. "He went out this way." Lazarus hurried to the elevator.

Lisa followed. She was most confused. "Please tell me what happened." she pleaded, quite disturbed.

"A man was in the garden. He belted me. I saw him go down the hall. At first I thought maybe he was a security officer."

"What did he look like?"

"It was all so fast, I couldn't give an accurate description." She turned and entered her bedroom.

Lazarus heard a scream and hurried to her. "What's wrong?"

"I have been robbed! My jewel box is gone."

Lazarus fumbled in his pockets. "Good Lord!" he exclaimed, "I left my pills at the hotel." He loosened his shirt collar. "I have to sit down." His voice became raspy, he looked up at her, "Do you have any heart pills?"

"No, I have no need for them."

He began to gasp. "Do you have a doctor in the building?"

"Yes," she said, "Dr. Fisk, on the fifth floor."

"Could you call him?" He started to fall back, stopped for a split second, turned to see where the chair was, then continued to fall back into the chair.

Lisa stood in momentary shock, then picked up the phone and dialed. "Doctor, this is Lisa Kinmore, there is an emergency up here. A gentleman is having a heart attack, I think. Hurry, please!" She hung up and rushed to Lazarus. "The doctor will be right up." She looked at him closer, his face was becoming pale. "Oh dear, you are not well! What can I do?"

Lazarus gave only a slight wave of his hand.

"Just hold on," she said tearfully, "the doctor is coming." There was the sound of the elevator door opening. She hurried to the hall. "He's in here, Doctor," she said, pointing and sobbing.

The doctor was wearing a robe over his pajamas, and he was carrying a black bag which he opened immediately, re-

48

moving his stethoscope. He opened Lazarus' shirt front and listened intently. Then he removed the instrument from his ears and hurried to the phone, and dialed. "Hello, paramedics. This is Dr. Fisk. I have an emergency—heart—the penthouse apartment, top floor of the Kinmore Building. Yes, please hurry!" He hung up the phone and moved quickly back to Lazarus. "They are in the neighborhood. Let's hope it's not too late." He broke a small capsule and sniffed it under his own nose. He listened to Lazarus' heart again, then turned to Lisa. "He is gone, I am sorry. Who is he?"

"A Mr. Larry King. I met him at Mrs. Kent's party tonight. He just stopped by a minute for a nightcap. On top of that, my place was robbed."

The doctor frisked the body. Lisa became angry. "What are you doing? This poor man had nothing to do with it, except trying to stop the man. The fright was too much for him." Suddenly, she gasped.

"Take it easy," said the doctor, "everything will be all right."

"Oh dear," she said, "a man dying in my apartment—and Dudley's death just a few months ago!" She was turning into a case of nerves.

"It's not your fault! These things happen," consoled the doctor.

"But the scandal! The gossip will ruin me socially."

"You'd better notify the police about the robbery," advised the doctor.

"Yes," she said as she started to the phone. But then she changed her mind. "No, just forget about the robbery."

"You have to report it or the insurance company won't cover the loss."

"It's all right."

"Good heavens, Lisa, your jewels must be worth a fortune!"

She showed signs of remorse. "Look, Doctor you are a good friend. I can't report the robbery. You see, I didn't list everything with the tax department for the inheritance tax. And Dudley didn't exactly get the jewels honestly."

The doctor reached into his robe pocket. "Maybe it's best you are not here when the medics arrive. Take my key, go down to my apartment and wait there. I'll take care of everything here."

She picked up her fur coat, purse, and overnight bag. He escorted her to the elevator and gave her the key to his apartment. As they waited for the elevator they heard the ambulance pulling up in front of the building.

The elevator opened and she got on. "What else is going to happen? First Dudley, now this."

"As soon as I get it cleared up here, I'll call you. If you need a sedative, I'll take care of that. Just get off at the fifth floor and don't worry."

The medics arrived a few minutes later. The two men with a stretcher were greeted at the door by the doctor. "I'm sure he is dead," he told them as he ushered them into the room.

One of the medics got defensive right away. "We got here as fast as we could."

The doctor assured him that it wasn't their fault.

When they reached Lazarus, the medic took a reading. "We do our best."

"And you do a good job."

The medic took out a report sheet. "Could you give me the man's name?"

"Mr. King, Mr. Larry King. Just take him to the morgue. I'll get dressed and be right down to fill out all the necessary forms."

They put Lazarus on the stretcher, covered him, strapped him on, then carried the body out. The medic stopped as the phone rang.

The doctor answered. "Yes, Lisa, they are just leaving." He paused, then said, "That's a good idea. You go to your place in the country. No need to come up here, I'll call you later. You drive carefully." He hung up the phone and saw the two men standing in the hall. "Something wrong?" asked the doctor.

50

"Shouldn't we notify the coroner or something?" the medic asked.

"What for? The man died, he wasn't murdered! You take him to the morgue. I'll follow in my car and meet you there."

"O.K., Doc, see you at the ice house." They headed toward the elevator with the body. The doctor entered the elevator, too, but he got off at the fifth floor.

Minutes later, the ambulance was shrilling through the street. A block away they turned onto a freeway ramp where they met with a traffic tie-up. Both medics leaned out of the ambulance doors trying to find a way through or out of the jam.

Meanwhile, Lazarus had fully recovered, saw the problem, unfastened the leather strap, scooted off the stretcher, opened the back door of the ambulance, and made his way through the congestion of yelling voices and blowing horns. He immediately headed back to the Kinmore Apartment building, found the back entrance and went up the freight elevator to the penthouse floor. Carefully, he entered the hall and tried the door. It was locked. Remembering the statue, he tilted it, got the key and let himself into the apartment. Cautiously, he walked through the hall, through the living room, out the door, into the garden. He retrieved the jewels, stuffed them into his pockets, wiped the box with his handkerchief, put the key back under the statue, then hurried back to the freight elevator and out of the building, unnoticed. His body was drenched with perspiration.

As he reached the street, he hailed a passing cab which took him to the Trymore Hotel. There was no one in sight as he entered the lobby elevator. He went to his room, picked up the phone and called the front desk. "Hello, this is Mr. Larry King. In ten minutes I'll be checking out. Will you put my bill in order, then call me and tell me the exact amount. I'll be paying in cash and don't like to flash money about." He hung up, checked out of the hotel, got into a cab and said, "Airport!" and flew to L.A.

Once in L.A., he just sort of disappeared into thick air.

51

CHAPTER FIVE

The reader is curious, perhaps, how I know so much about The Great Lazarus. Well, as I mentioned already, he intrigued me so much that I spent much time and effort pursuing leads and following his trail in order to find out as much about him as I could. Further, through the episodes such as those described I became a trusted friend. Over the years, through his own testimony and that of others I was able to piece together his incredible story.

I must admit that I admired him very much even though I didn't approve of some of the things he did. And he trusted me and knew that I would not publish my book about him until he decided to reach beyond that unaggravated quietness of calm, peaceful tranquility where he would learn the full meaning of trance and the outmost limit of life.

I discovered at one point that he had married for a second time. When I eventually saw his wife in photographs, I knew he had gone the limit, not in life, but to carry out some con game. It must have been to get part of her wealth because she was nothing remotely close to the vision he so trusted. That was the vision he spoke of in my initial interview with him when he told me what it was like to return to life from one of his trances, the vision of the lady who was like blue smoke from a candle just extinguished. With her deep sapphire-blue eyes, her pirouetting form, she took his hand each time he returned to life and floated him through this long tunnel into the light. That vision was his mother, who had died at childbirth.

By some strange mystery he had total recall of his birth and his mother. That is why I knew his marriage to Sarah Halstead Graham was no more than a set-up for some scam.

Sarah Halsted was her maiden name, Graham came from her previous husband. There had been three others before him. She had a strange quirk for elderly men—two of whom had died from being "overweight." They were covered heavily by insurance, and there was significant community property. She converted most of her assets to jewelry, which she believed to be a safe investment. In case of war or when traveling, gems can be sewn into the lining or hems of skirts, where they will never be discovered.

Sarah was rather buxom, but youthful in appearance, especially her angelic face. Her language, however, was crude and, sometimes even, vulgar. Overall, she wasn't particularly appealing, even though she may have been more attractive in her youth. But by the time she married Lazarus she had developed all the attributes that made a perfect blueprint, if someone wished to build a bore.

Thirty-five years old when Lazarus first met her, she had married her first husband at age eighteen, while she was working as a waitress in Dallas. He was in oil, she was in a bathing suit—a passionate combination that seemed to coagulate immediately. But something went wrong. She saw his will, he saw her with a young lover. In fact, he had followed her. Sarah knew she was on the way out of his will, so she and her boyfriend arranged a going-away party that her husband wouldn't know about.

His name was J. Worthington Haggens, and he was sixty-seven years old. After discovering her infidelity he made an appointment with his lawyer to change his will and to cancel a two hundred thousand dollar insurance policy that named Sarah as beneficiary. On Sunday, before his Monday morning appointment with his lawyer, Haggens met with an accident. He fell off his polo pony and broke his neck. Sarah decided it was nothing more than a little whiplash and didn't bother to call the doctor.

She received half the estate and all the insurance money. So that there would be no contesting of the will, she settled with the family. They bought her part of the estate for one million dollars in cash, plus an annuity of one hundred thousand a year for five years. Sarah became a rich widow, but also a lonely one.

So a month later she looked for and found another elderly gentleman—Willy Fenton, age sixty-four. She took out an insurance policy on him for three hundred thousand, just as if it were part of the marriage vows. He soon caught a virus with a corrupting influence—it was called "money." He became weaker as his medication got stronger. The medication was a chemical called arsenic that was given to Sarah by a boyfriend in medical school. The student also taught her there was no way of tracing the effects of arsenic. Sarah, being a faithful wife, stayed with Willy night and day until the special medication took effect. After it did, the will was read and Sarah's wealth greatly increased.

Once again, she invested her money in rare gems, which made her collection worth over three million dollars. This interest in jewels led Sarah to her next husband, a diamond merchant named Jim Fillmore. He was fifty-one and had just lost his wife. Sarah knew how to comfort him through their mutual interest in jewelry. They tied the knot, or, I should say, noose around his neck. A year later Sarah had that urge for young romance again, and she started playing around. This time with a weightlifter, a real body beautiful. She would go up to his weight reducing parlor because she wanted to lose about 180 pounds—her husband. He wasn't happy about all of this, and when he learned that she had taken out a half million dollar insurance policy on him and he heard the nasty rumors about her other husbands, he divorced her by working out a settlement that included a sixty carat ruby, a sixty-five carat sapphire, a thirty carat diamond and a forty carat emerald. She worshipped the emerald and, when she didn't wear it, she carried it in her purse. She felt it was her good luck charm.

Lazarus saw her several times at parties, but showed no interest in her. It was love at first sight, however, when he saw the gems that decorated her pudgy body. She looked like the storeroom for the Kimberly Diamond Mines of South Africa. Sarah thought him to be handsome, witty, and exciting. He was always with a different woman at every party and she couldn't stand to see other women with such an interesting man. She just had to meet him. So she gave a party and invited Mr. Larry Williams, the handsome man with the beard.

Lazarus knew of her affection for emeralds. She would make an easy mark. He visited his safety deposit box, took out a fifty-five carat emerald, put it in his pocket, then formally accepted her party invitation.

While the guests waited for Sarah to make her grand entrance, Lazarus enjoyed the string quartet playing waltzes by Skelton, and a young Lady violinist playing "Butterfly." He studied Sarah's collection of oil paintings, which were colorful and expensive. Some were fakes, given away to the trained eye by their perfection. He also watched the guests, especially one, a dapper old gent over eighty. He was well-tailored but his hands were as rough as a stoker glove. The veins at his temples were swollen like a run-away horse. His complexion was yellowish green with a light purplish tint, especially around his lips and nose. His eyes were barely visible through his thin half-closed lids. It made him look both depressed and half asleep.

Lazarus introduced himself, for the old gent seemed not only alone, but out of place. "I am Larry Williams," he said as he extended his hand.

"Shrewsbury," said the old gent. "I don't think we have met before. What's your business?"

"I am an author."

"Ah, that Williams. I've read your books."

He knew Shrewsbury was just making talk because Lazarus had never even written a check, let alone a book.

"Well," continued the old man, "I was a writer back in 1920. You look healthy."

"Never been in the hospital."

"Really?" said Shrewsbury. "What the hell do you talk about?" After he gave a little laugh, he went on, "I went to the blood bank today, but they wouldn't give me any."

Lazarus looked at him. "I thought you were going to say you gave them all your blood."

"I used to do that, but no more. The last time I gave blood, they put a label on the bottle: 'Artificial Coloring to be Added.' The last time I gave blood was back in 1910." The old gent backed away and squinted, as if he were trying to bring Lazarus into focus. "Say, you are a nice looking fellow. What are you doing at this party alone? You ought to mill around and find a good looker. Are you married?"

"No, I'm not."

"Well, you are better off. I was married, but my wife ran away with the black chauffeur."

"Oh!"

"Yeah, but it's my own fault. I should have never married a black woman to begin with."

Lazarus looked at the old man, not knowing what to make of him or his comments.

"Yep, and that was something you seldom heard of back in 1910."

"You know," said Lazarus, eager to get away, "I'm going to take your advice and mill around."

Lazarus started to walk away, as he wished to be alone. But as he looked up he had the feeling that a rather lofty lady was about to latch onto him. He turned a pretended to be admiring a statue of Pam, but, as fate would have it, the amazon nailed him.

"That's rather dark," she commented, looking at his glass. "May I ask what you are drinking?"

"Ice tea. Shall I order you some?"

"No, but if you'll get me a scotch and soda, I'll force it down."

Lazarus called a servant girl over. "Could you bring the lady a scotch and soda—double?"

The lady then introduced herself. "I am Esther Lane."

"I am Larry Williams."

"I've never seen you at any of Sarah's parties before."

Lazarus lowered his glass. "I've never been at one of her parties before." He then escorted her to a couch, turned, and took the drink from the tray the servant girl was holding. Handing the glass to the lady, he started to sit, but hesitated and asked, "Do you mind if I sit next to you?"

"Please do," she responded as she took a long sip of her drink. "Do you like parties?"

"To be truthful, no. Parties are like rituals—no fun. You waste time talking to people who mean nothing to you, and unless you exchange some inside gossip about the host or a guest, some spicy chit-chat, there is no pleasure at all. You just wind up getting potted and becoming a wallflower. If you do gossip you transform yourself into a human information booth. Then, if by some unfortunate chance, you are confronted by the person you have mocked or slandered, all ears become receivers and all accusing eyes become beacons. No one ever comes to your rescue by saying in your defense, 'My, he certainly made you sound like an exciting person.' "

"Isn't that the truth," said Mrs. Lane, handing Lazarus her empty glass. "Would you be a nice gentleman and get me another one of these? Tell them to leave out the ice and soda."

"How about I just get the bottle and you can fix it the way you like it?"

She looked at Lazarus. "Don't get me wrong, but you have to fortify yourself for Sarah. You know, I've got a problem. I saw my husband going into a theater with another woman. I would have gone in after them, but I had already seen the movie." She swallowed a chuckle.

Lazarus got up and went to the bar. He asked the bartender, "Have you got a stein back there?"

"Yes. You don't expect a lady to drink out of a bottle, do you?" Lazarus returned with a eight ounce glass filled with straight scotch.

Mrs. Lane laughed. "Aren't you a darling."

"There you are. Drink up, be somebody."

"Thank you. Now, you were saying something very interesting about parties." She took a long sip, then sat back. "I don't remember what you said, but you know, you are right."

"Right about what?"

"About idle chatter. For instance, there are folks here I could write a book about. It would make me interesting for a moment."

Lazarus replied, "You will excuse me, there is something I have to do."

"Go right ahead. Maybe we can talk again later. By the way, Mr. Williams, what business are you in?"

"For fifteen years I worked for the government—five years in Atlanta, ten in Levenworth." As he excused himself, he thought, "She is a lovely lady. The type you'd like to see through a rear view mirror." He walked over to an oil painting and searched for the artist's signature. Suddenly, there was a murmur in the room as Sarah made her grand entrance, leaving a bad taste in everyone's eyes.

Upon seeing Lazarus she excused herself and walked over to him. She extended her hand. "Well, at last we meet." He kept staring at the painting and did not see her hand. "Are you enjoying yourself?" she inquired.

"Not really. Parties are non-productive—a hang-out for a

bunch of freeloaders with spoiled appetites who eat over-cooked food and become candidates for dyspepsia."

Sarah gave him a most seductive, yet coy, glance. "My," she said, "such flattery! If you dislike them so much, why did you come?"

"When I saw the dainty signature on the invitation, I couldn't pass up the opportunity to meet the woman who it belonged to." Then, seeing it was Sarah, but not letting on that he knew who it was, he took her hand and gave it a squeeze. "But after meeting you, I don't even care if I meet the hostess." He stared at Sarah, then looked at the painting and became most embarrassed. "Oh, I'm sorry, it's you. But that portrait does absolutely nothing for your beauty." He could see that she was more than flattered. "You know neither that painting nor the photographs in the newspapers do you justice, at all. May I get you something to drink?"

"No, thank you, I believe it's just about time for dinner."

As Sarah made her grand entrance into the dining room with Lazarus in tow, he immediately saw that it was a set-up. She had arranged the table so that he would be seated to her right. During the dinner he turned on the charm, but she found the food more exciting. She never stopped eating.

He did find a moment to call attention to her jewelry. For this occasion she was decorated in the worst taste. She had on long earrings, a necklace, and bracelets, all of which were so lavish that they distracted one from noticing her gaudy hairdo and make-up, which was so heavy she should have been wearing a 'WET PAINT' sign. "You will pardon me for being rude, but I must admire your emerald," said Lazarus as he took her hand. As soon as he touched it she could feel vibrations from him. He looked at the ring. "It is beautiful. Seems that we both admire emeralds," he said, reaching into his pocket and bringing out his emerald ring.

She almost choked on her food when she saw the fifty-five carats of perfection. "Oh, my God! It is beautiful. I don't want to be rude or vulgar, but what did a little sucker like that set you back? Look at the garden in that stone!" She sat eyeing the emerald like a vulture over a fresh kill, but she still called the servant to serve her more meat.

Lazarus tried to pick up the conversation with the same enthusiasm. "You were referring to the price of the stone. I couldn't even estimate a guess. It was given to me by the Maharajah of Gadeor."

"Where is Gadeor?"

"In India."

"India," repeated Sarah, now overcome with a fake, dreamy Pola Negri melodramic swoon. "I've always wanted to go there!" Then she called for more rolls and butter.

"They would love you in India."

"Why me?"

"They love beautiful women. In fact, in India you would be sacred," he said, giving her fat body a once-over glance as she fondled the ring.

"It seems so alive," she said.

Again, Lazarus tried to take control of the direction of the conversation. "I find gems most fascinating. I made a study of the history of gems and their legends, such as the Hope Diamond which is now in the Smithsonian. And I discovered there is only one stone that has only good mythology and sound connection with legend. That is the emerald. It always brings good luck to its owner. There is one emerald somewhere in the world that Alexander the Great carried and it gave him the strength to conquer the world. But it was stolen from him and when next heard of, it turned up in Hannibal's possession. It was that emerald, not his will, that gave him the courage to cross the Alps with elephants. That stone has hundreds of legends connected to it."

"Well," said Sarah, handing the ring back to him. "Oh God, I think I ate too much!" Then she pointed to the ring and said, "If you ever want to sell that little sucker, let me know."

"With a lovely lady like you," said Lazarus, again holding her hand, "the price wouldn't be too much." He slowly slipped the ring on her pinky finger, and then quickly removed it.

She thought for a second, then, under her breath, said, "I see what you mean."

Lazarus only responded with a bashful smile.

The party came to an end early. Sarah had eaten so much, nothing fit; she had to get comfortable. At the door, Lazarus was saying good night. He asked if she could have one of her servants call him a cab.

"You don't have a car?"

"For safety reasons, I don't drive. You see, I am a writer and, at times, my mind is on something other than the traffic."

Sarah became interested. "I was going to ask what your racket was. What are some of your books?"

"One is *Hypotenuse of the Planet Mars*. My latest is *The Measurement of the Fifth Ring Around the Planet Venus*."

"You write that science fiction stuff?"

"Not fiction, aerospace facts. I did one fiction—*Ten Ways to Cheat at Polo!*"

"Well, I don't want to insult you, but I don't think I could understand that deep stuff. I have to struggle to get through 'Cosmopoliton.' "

"You are joking," replied Lazarus with a chuckle. "I saw your library."

"Oh yeah," she said, "they came with the house. The whole top row are fakes."

Lazarus shook his head. "You have great simplicity and wonderful honesty," said Lazarus, giving her hand enough squeeze to let her feel the emerald ring again.

"Look," said Sarah, "I'll have my chauffeur drive you where you want to go. No need for you to take a cab."

"Thank you. Are you sure it's not an imposition?"

"No, no." She turned to the maid who was handing coats to the guests. "Velma, go tell Victor to get the Rolls out and take Mr. Williams to the Plaza Towers."

"They have wonderful food at the hotel. Would you have dinner with me tomorrow evening?"

She patted her stomach. "After what I put away tonight, I shouldn't eat for a week."

"In case you change your mind, here is my card."

She gave him a knowing glance. "I know your address. I mailed your invitation."

While Lazarus was putting on his overcoat, he was greeted by the curious old gentleman, Mr. Shrewsbury. "It was a lovely party, but this knocking about and the late hour are slowing me down. This was like the parties we used to give—everybody whoever did anybody attended. I gave a party once that went three days and nights. Let's see, that was back in . . .."

Lazarus, thinking he might help him out, said, "1910."

The old fellow looked at him and said, "No, that was in 1934."

•   •   •

The next day at ten in the morning, Lazarus sent a bouquet of twenty-four red and white roses to Sarah's home. There was no response, but Lazarus knew she like to play hard to get. So, for the next few days, Lazarus continued to send gifts to Sarah with notes of gratitude for the delightful amusement she afforded him at her party. They were nice gifts, in various forms—one, a leather gold-trimmed daily reference book with an inscription on each page, "Dinner Tonight." A week later she received one flower with a note that wasn't flattering, but it struck her funny. It read: "I saw you at distance. There was something about you that was different. I searched my mind and then it came to me why you looked so lovely. You had shaved." It was so humorous.

That night they had dinner together. One week after a whirlwind romance, their engagement was announced. A week later they were married—only because her horoscope predicted that she should.

She said it was love at first sight. But the love at first sight took that second look and diminished their romance in record time. Sarah didn't get the emerald as a wedding present, even though she thought she could talk him out of it. Within a month she was back to her old habits with college boys.

One day she brought in papers for Lazarus to sign. It was an insurance policy for a half a million dollars. Lazarus refused, saying he'd never live to see the money. But after a week of nagging, he consented. She agreed to pay for the insurance if she were the beneficiary.

It was during a dinner dance at the Beach Club that Lazarus discovered Sarah was really hung up on the life guard. Lazarus was seated behind some ferns when he overheard Sarah talking to her boy friend. Up to that moment he was exceedingly ignorant about what was going on. Sarah had been drinking and she didn't realize her voice was so loud. "I tell you, I am getting rid of him," she said, "but you've got to help me. That is, unless you don't want to get married." She then gave the boy a passionate kiss.

The young man was nervous. "I can't give you anything. I am poor, you are a rich lady," said the young man.

"So what's there to worry about? That prune I am married to doesn't give me anything. So as long as I am not getting anything, why shouldn't I have fun?" With that remark she grabbed the young man and kissed him again, saying, "I want you. I need youth around me to feel I am alive."

Lazarus said nothing about what he had heard. But he knew the plot would soon be reaching the point where she would be mixing him a bye-bye cocktail. Lazarus knew it was getting very close when Sarah hired the young man as a security guard and put him in the upstairs' bedroom.

A few days later Lazarus was looking for a cuff link that rolled under the bed. He found not only the cuff link, but a wire attached to a microphone. He traced the wire and discovered it connected to a receiver in the quest room. The device allowed Sarah to hear if Lazarus was awake when she wanted to sneak into the young man's room during the night.

Lazarus went to an electrical shop and bought some recording equipment one afternoon while the young man was driving Sarah on a shopping spree to buy new clothes for her young lover. Lazarus hooked up a cordless mike in the young man's room, placed it under the bed, and, then put the receiver in his own room, attached to a recorder.

That night, about one A.M., Lazarus heard Sarah open her door. He peeked out and saw her going into the young man's room. He hurried and put on his earphones, and listened to and recorded their conversation. At the same time, into the mike under his bed he played a recording of someone snoring. He knew they would hear the snoring and, believing Lazarus to be asleep, would feel free to talk. And they did.

"Do you think we will get away with killing your husband?" asked the young man.

Sarah was most convincing. "There is no way they can trace this poison. I got rid of two husbands and there was no evidence."

"It seems awfully cruel. Why don't you just divorce him?"

"What, and ruin my social standing!" exclaimed Sarah. "Besides, insurance companies don't pay for divorces. Look, it worked in Texas and Missouri."

"When are you going to do it?" asked the young man, who still didn't seem too sure of her idea.

"In a few days. I've got to get the arsenic."

The next morning Lazarus didn't know what to expect. He drank water from the garden hose and didn't eat any breakfast. He walked through the garden and out the side gate where a cab, he had previously called, picked him up. He went to a little lunch room where he ate breakfast. While eating and reading the newspaper he saw an advertisement announcing the opening of the state fair. There was a picture of Thelma the Mystic, who was one of the attractions at the fair. He thought for a moment, paid his check, hired a cab, and went to the fairgrounds.

The smell of the sawdust, hot dogs and other outdoor food

reminded him of his earlier, happy days with the carnival. As he walked down the midway he enjoyed the sight of the ferris wheel, merry-go-round, the little ball-pitching stands with the stuffed animals, the haunted house, the side show, and the girlie show. Suddenly, he came to the tent of Thelma the Mystic.

After many years she had finally elevated her spot from platform act in a side show to her own tent. She charged two dollars for the crystal ball reading, three dollars for a private reading. Lazarus stopped and looked at Thelma, who was dressed in a beautiful gypsy costume. The tent was decorated with oriental rugs. On top of a lovely teakwood table was her crystal ball, and next to the table were two ornate, hand-carved chairs, huge brass incense burners, and a portable air conditioner. Thelma was seated in a large, high-backed chair. Lazarus stood looking at her. Age had left its wrinkles, and folds gathered loosely about her body, which seemed no more than a trellis for dry skin to hang from. She seemed unnerved by his staring and asked him, using a thick accent from some country not yet discovered, "Would you like to know of the future?"

Lazarus laughed. "Why you old fake, you can't even remember the past."

Thelma became annoyed. "Move along, buster," she said angrily.

"Hey, don't you recognize me, Thelma? It's me, The Great Lazarus."

She stared at him for a second. Then walked to him and threw her arms around him. It was the warmest welcome he had received in some time. "Dear friend, how are you? My, we thought you had died!" She smiled. "I mean that you had died for real. What a horrible thing to say."

"It's O.K. How good to see you after all these years," said Lazarus, warmly.

She opened the flap to the tent. "Gerald, hurry, come out here!"

Gerald must have thought there was a problem. He came out with a ball bat and looked sternly at Lazarus. "What's the problem?" he asked.

"Howdy, Gerald."

"Hi," he answered coldly, tapping the bat into the palm of his hand.

"It's The Great Lazarus!" exclaimed Thelma.

Gerald dropped the ball bat right on Lazarus, stood close, gave Lazarus a big embrace, backed away, then hugged him again, all the while becoming very emotional. "Oh, it's good to see you! We have often thought of you. What an attraction you were! What are you doing here?"

"I came to visit with you."

Thelma offered him a chair, then, with reverence, she said, "We did think you were dead."

Lazarus smiled. "You already said that."

Gerald sat down and said, "Lazarus, you old devil. That chair is hard. You want a cushion? Make yourself at home." After another admiring glance, he said, "I knew it was you the minute I saw you, but I wasn't sure."

Lazarus laughed. "She is the mind reader and you do the remembering."

"Well, you know how it is," she said, "you get old and everything becomes a rumor."

"You look good, Gerald," complimented Lazarus.

"I should," he said, stretching himself. "I just got out of the hospital. Nothing trivial. Six doctors removed my bankbook."

"What can we get you?" asked Thelma.

"How about me treating you both to a hot dog?" replied Lazarus.

"Oh dear, he hasn't changed. He still loves those hot dogs." Thelma looked at him. "You sure look prosperous and healthy. Doesn't he look good, Gerald?"

Gerald smiled. "He sure does."

"How are you folks doing?" inquired Lazarus.

"Not too good since television came in. A fortune teller hasn't a chance with all the newscasters predicting the future. There's no news anymore, just opinions and predictions. It's getting more communistic everyday. They tell you what they want to put in your mind. I've got the feeling that freedom of the press is going to do away with all the freedoms." Thelma stopped for a breath.

"You married yet?" asked Gerald.

"Yeah."

"Any children?"

"No, only married a little over a year. She is a body beautiful."

Thelma noticed there was something wrong. "You don't seem too happy for a newlywed," she said, in a way that asked for an answer.

"To tell the truth, I'm not. She likes to play around."

Thelma wasn't sure if he was joking. "You are serious?"

"Yeah, I saw her going into this guy's room and she left the keyhole open."

"Oh, no!"

"Yeah, she and this young buck are planning to knock me off."

"Maybe you just imagine it. Why would anyone want to knock you off?"

"Money," said Lazarus, with a reassuring pat on Gerald's knee. "She just took out a half a million dollar policy on me."

"I've never believed in insurance. They keep you poor so you can die with a little money," said Gerald.

"We have group insurance with the show," said Thelma, disgustedly. "That means we get money if we all die as a group. Half a million, eh? It takes a lot of money to buy a policy like that."

"She's got it. But I plan a little heist myself," he said most confidently. "I am getting ready to do my act again. That's why I came to see you folks. You have a chance to make five thousand dollars from me and maybe even more from her."

"Well, we have always tried to stay clean," said Thelma. "Least thing and the police close us down."

"No problem. She is a real nut on horoscopes and spiritualism. I'm sure she'll fall for what I have in mind."

"A real yokel," commented Gerald, shaking his head.

"Please," said Thelma, "you are biting the crystal ball that feeds me. But what do you have in mind?"

Lazarus thought a moment, then pulled his chair close to them. "You are friends, so I can tell you. She is insane about jewelry. She has to have about three million dollars worth of it. She has one emerald, a beauty. I made up a story about a famous emerald that had great power. Supposedly, it disappeared years ago. But it had power like the Holy Grail. It could grant wishes. Now, I plan on having a party—a gypsy party. You folks will be invited. You tell a few fortunes, and when you come to Sarah—that's my wife—you put on the old, 'I can't tell you what I see in the crystal ball' routine. Then you tell her you see the missing emerald, that she has it, and that is has so much power. The owner could wish someone dead. If the stone were near that person, he or she would die."

"Sort of the old drop, without the package," said Gerald.

"Sort of. You tell her that the more gems with the emerald, the more powerful it becomes. You tell her nations have been conquered with its power. Tell her that you see in the ball some plans to murder her husband."

"I don't know? Sounds like a chance to meet with the bunko squad," said Gerald, very concerned.

"All you have to do is plant in her mind that the emerald has power. Convince her that all anyone would have to do is put a bag of jewels and the emerald under the victim's bed and make a wish and they are absolved of responsibility. The power of the emerald does it."

Thelma said, "Sounds far-fetched, but I could work out something."

Gerald spoke with enthusiasm. "It's a cinch! When do you want to pull this off?"

69

"Well, give me a few days. The fair runs how long?"

"Who cares?" said Thelma. "If I get my hands on five thousand dollars, we are blowing this pop stand. We have a little place outside Paso Robles, California. You know, I am getting too old for living like a gypsy."

Lazarus reached for his wallet. "To show good faith. I have two thousand with me, but I'll give you the other three at the party. Meantime, I'll hire a press agent to get your picture and story in the paper. That will help convince my wife how great you are. In fact, you'll be the greatest since Nostradamis."

Two days later, Lazarus opened the paper at the breakfast table and handed it to Sarah.

"Here is something that should be of interest to you. Thelma the Mystic is at the fair."

"Who is Thelma?"

"You are joking? She is the one who predicted that Amelia Earhart would disappear, and she even gave the day. She also predicted, in 1931, that America would be the first to land men on the moon, even gave the date it would happen."

Sarah read the article.

"You know what might be a novel idea? Let's give a gypsy party," suggested Lazarus, "and invite Thelma. It would be different, and it could be the social event of the year. Great entertainment, everyone would come to hear what predictions she makes. You know, Issac Stern is in town. We can invite him, have gypsy singers and dancers and violins. I'll get right on it."

"What would a thing like that cost?" Sarah wondered.

"Look, Sarah, you never let me do things. Let me show you I am not all that dull. Besides, you like that fortune telling stuff. Why not hear from the greatest?"

The party *was* the social event of the season. It cost Lazarus twenty thousand dollars, but he figured it was insurance that gave him time not only to save his life but to pull the biggest caper of his career.

The estate lawn was covered with tents, bars, singers, dancers, and violinists playing gypsy music. There were dancing bears, shish kabab, rare wines, string quartets, and extra servants in colorful costumes. The champagne corks popped like the Fourth of July. Each lady guest received a pair of golden earrings. The men received Russian leather wallets. And the main attraction was Thelma the Mystic. After a reading, she gave each guest their own crystal ball. The only mystery about them was why they were made by Pittsburgh Glass.

Sarah was decked out as a gypsy princess. Because of the jewelry she was wearing, there were special armed security police, and special generators ready to take over should someone tamper with the main power switch.

Thelma was most impressive. She realized this was the highlight of her career. All the attention was far beyond her expectations and she played her part to the hilt, reading palms, and truly making guests feel they had been told their destiny, though, at times, she saw nothing in the hands of those who came to her.

At the entrance, Polaroid pictures were taken of the guests. They were rushed to Gerald who, with his list of guests and photos of all of them, stood behind a two-way mirror and told Thelma who each guest was. His directional microphone reached the earphones hidden under Thelma's turban, and this helped considerably to enhance her mystic powers. If Gerald misidentified someone, Thelma said, "I feel a disturbance with the spirit. I cannot tell you anything."

Lazarus stood by Thelma's tent and gave each guest a gold coin to cross Thelma's palm with—a traditional gypsy demand. There were a few non-believers who took the gold coin and crossed their own palms.

After awhile, Sarah could no longer contain her curiosity. She approached The Great Thelma, who took Sarah's hand, then, with a mysterious observation, and held the one finger that was circled by the emerald ring. Thelma made a few passes over the ball with her hand. Then, after looking into it with horror, she quickly covered the ball with a black velvet cloth. Then she studied the ring and looked at the amazed expression on Sarah's face. When Thelma put the back of her hand to her forehead, in a most dramatic fashion, Sarah became concerned. "What is wrong?" she asked.

Thelma backed away, then said, "I didn't see anything. I can't tell you anything." Then she got up from her throne-like chair and walked away as if disturbed.

Sarah was embarrassed AND angry. She stopped Thelma. "You did see something in that ball." Thelma held her hands up and shook her head. Sarah became angry. "I am paying you for this service, I want to know what you saw!"

Thelma looked at her and said, "Better you do not know. Best you be full of concern, than face reality."

Sarah again stopped Thelma from walking away. "You saw something. I want to know what it is."

"I saw something. It was like figures standing in the sun, but there were no shadows."

"Is that bad?"

Thelma pulled herself away from Sarah's grip. "It isn't good." Then, seeing that Sarah was persistent, Thelma picked up her glass ball, then asked, "Is there some place we can go that is private?"

"Yes, my den." The two ladies walked through the festivities into the house and to the den. "There, sit at my desk," Sarah said, pointing to a huge handcarved desk.

Thelma put the ball on the desk, closed her eyes, then said, "The emerald ring, where did you get it?"

"What's that got to do with what you saw—and I know you saw something?"

"First, the ring."

"What about it?"

"Do not push it aside like it was nothing. You are in possession of the most valuable emerald in the world. It's importance has been passed on through the centuries. At one time, if the gypsy nation could have gained possession of that emerald, we would now be the ruling class of the world. It's a sacred gem. It was in the breastplate worn by Moses."

Sarah was doubtful. She turned her head slightly, but didn't take her eyes off Thelma. Suddenly Sarah remembered what Lazarus had said about the lost emerald. "You mean this ring is that stone?"

"I am certain," said Thelma, as if she were frightened of the ring. "It has powers beyond belief."

"What did you see in that giant marble?" asked Sarah.

"Now, what I saw in the crystal ball, I do not know if the spirits will return." She gazed into the ball. She then spoke in a low voice. Even Ethel Barrymore couldn't have given a better—or more convincing—performance. "The ball is becoming misty. There is a black haze. Now there is a green figure standing. I cannot make out a face, it's all too misty. I see a murder, not a violent murder, but one by a liquid, a poison. There are two people involved. A young man, he holds the hand of the other figure. They stand over the body. It's not clear. Then the one figure waves a green light. No, no. It's the emerald! Its power commits the murder. Now the figure of a woman is free because of her control over the mystic power of the emerald. I can tell you no more." Thelma covered the ball and fell back into her chair, as if exhausted.

"Tell me more about the emerald!" Sarah shouted.

Thelma pretended she was trying to obey and commanded Sarah to, "Ask your questions before I lose my trance. For once I return, I remember nothing that's been said."

"You said the emerald kills the victim."

"Yes, it has that power over all living things."

"So the emerald's power commits the murder?"

"If it was the wish of its master. Its master goes free, for she didn't kill, so cannot be held guilty." Then Thelma opened her eyes. "I can tell you no more," she said in a raspy voice. Then Thelma slowly raised her head. "You must now help me. You have more mystic power than I do." Thelma covered the ball more securely, then she took Sarah's hand. "Dear Lady," she said, most tenderly, "I am not going to hoodwink you. True, I have the power to see into the future, and I admit a little showmanship in my performance. I don't know what I told you, but it was the truth. When I go that much into the spirit world I can't remember what I said once I return from the trance. I'll be honest with you. You may not know it, but you have in your possession the most powerful stone in the world! It can be compared to the Holy Grail."

"The Holy Grail?"

"Yes, the emerald was one of the stones in Moses' breast-plate. Read Exodus, verses 1 through 40. Any wish you make will come true. If you were to surround that emerald with other precious stones, the power it would have would be staggering. The more you surround it with other stones, the more power it has. Well, look what Napoleon did with it. He placed it in satchels in the middle of a country and the country was conquered with a wish, and without guilt. Did you ever wonder why he was sent into exile? He wasn't a war criminal. The emerald was. I venture to say, men have been murdered and the master of the emerald went free. After all, you can't send an emerald to jail and it's always the stone that carries out the death wish. To destroy the stone would cause a religious war." Thelma stopped and gave a wave of her hand. "Please, I am very tired, I can't tell you any more." She closed her eyes, shook her head, as if to shake off some strain. "I have never gone so far under before. Did I tell you anything important?" she asked Sarah.

"Don't you remember?" Sarah asked her.

"When I go into a trance, I only repeat what the spirits tell me. I don't remember one word I said once I lose contact." She glanced at Sarah to see if she was buying her line.

"You couldn't repeat anything to anyone, even my husband?"

Thelma displayed surprise. "You are married?"

Sarah smiled. "What do I owe you?"

"Anything in gold or silver, but cash will do. I can pick up something in gold or silver later."

"I'll give you your fee for tonight." Sarah unlocked the desk drawer, opened a small package and counted out twenty one hundred dollar bills. As they were walking out of the room they met Lazarus. Sarah said to him, "I'll be right back. It was very interesting."

Lazarus moved close to Thelma who was trailing behind. "Did she go for it?" he whispered.

"Hook, line, and sinker," she whispered back.

Sarah turned around and Thelma quickly said, "I've had an exhausting trauma. I couldn't give any other reading." She took a quick leave as Lazarus and Sarah bid her good night. Thelma hurried to Gerald, who was already in the car, packed and ready to go. She said to Gerald, "Let's get out of here, that's the easiest money we've ever earned."

Sarah was certain that she had the secret to a perfect crime. No more fear of investigation. No purchases at the drug store or garden shop. Many thoughts were spinning in her warped mind. She thought to herself, "I knew there was a reason I liked that emerald so much. If only I had known of its power, Haggins wouldn't have had those terrible throwing-up spells from that poison."

After all the guests were gone and the entertainers were paid and dismissed, Sarah expressed a desire to retire immediately, claiming the party had exhausted her.

Lazarus understood. "I know how you feel, dear, but it was a nice party, I think. I'm going to sit by the pool and relax." (In fact, he wanted to give her time to prepare for her big wish.)

He was so right. Sarah went to her double safe and took out three trays of her best gem stones. She wanted to give the little emerald all the help it would need, for she knew Lazarus was a strong fellow. She thought for a moment, "What if this is a joke? Well, what have I got to lose? If it doesn't work, there is always the old way. Besides, the gems will be safer under Lazarus' bed because he is too old and lazy to ever bend over and look under the bed. After all, he didn't discover the microphone." So she put two million dollars worth of gem stones in a small leather satchel, removed the emerald from her finger and placed it on top of the other jewels. Then, cat-like, she crept into his room and placed the satchel of gems under his bed. Then, as an act of affection (to cover her tracks), she turned down the bed covers for Lazarus as she heard him coming into the room.

"What is this?" he asked, seeing Sarah fluffing up the pillows.

"Just a little wifely duty. I had so much fun tonight, I wanted to do something to say, 'Thanks.' So I turned down the bed covers and laid out your pajamas."

"Thank you," said Lazarus. "It's a big bed," he said, trying to get a gleam in his eye.

"You dickens," she said, with a girlish giggle. "If I wasn't so exhausted, I'd get what you mean, but I am even too tired to even have a headache." She kissed her index finger, then touched his lips. "Good night," she said.

She left the room and Lazarus knew what he would find if he looked under the bed. He did, and it was there. An hour later, Lazarus called for Sarah. Like a flash, she was in his room. "I've got strange chest pains," he complained to her. "Best we send for the doctor."

Instead, she sent for the young security guard, who came into the room, all eyes. "Aren't you going to send for the doctor?"

"No, he's going on a little trip, and I don't mean to grand-mother's summer camp," replied Sarah.

At five in the morning, Lazarus started to gasp for air. "Why doesn't the doctor come?" he mumbled.

The young man said, "Mr. Williams, I called the doctor. He is on his way over."

All Sarah could think of was the emerald. It was working. But her thoughts were interrupted by the sound of a car pulling into the driveway. "Who is that?" asked Sarah, going to the window and looking at the car approaching the house.

"It must be the doctor," said the young man.

Sarah was furious. "You mean you really called the doctor, you idiot?"

"Yes, Mam, I had to," answered the young man, showing his fear. "Mam, what has gotten into you? Money is great to have, but not your way."

"No! snapped Sarah, "fresh air is the greatest thing. I think you better get some now. Get out of my sight!" shouted Sarah, as she gave him a shove. "Get out of here!"

"Note until the doctor gets here. I am sick of your greed."

Sarah calmed down when she saw the doctor was at the door.

It was then Lazarus gave the best performance of his life. The young man quickly gave him artificial respiration. The doctor took over shortly after he entered the room. After a few minutes he listened to Lazarus' heart, then slowly backed away and covered Lazarus' face. "He is dead," announced the doctor. "Why didn't you call earlier?"

Sarah then went into her performance, which was greatly overacted. The lady servants came, dressed in their robes and hair curlers, and tried to calm Sarah. The doctor took her by the arm and led her, wailing, from the room.

The young man addressed her in the hall. "I'll go pack my things."

When they all left, Lazarus slowly revived himself, and opened his eyes. As soon as he was sure he was alone, he got his suitcase and gathered up all the gems. Then, unnoticed, he sneaked down the backstairs and made his way to the side gate, where he checked his watch. Very shortly, Thelma and Gerald drove up. He put his bags into their vehicle and off they drove.

When the undertaker arrived, the excitment was tremendous as they started searching the bedroom for the body. Sarah was in shock. She cleared everyone out of the bedroom and practically dove under the bed. All she found was her satchel, empty except for a recording and a note.

Dear,

I hope you play this recording. It's most interesting; it deals with fraud and contains a confession admitting to the murder of two husbands. You explain how you served an arsenic cocktail to them. If you, in any way, attempt to find me, I will send a duplicate of this recording to the D.A.'s office in the two states where you committed the other crimes.

You are not an interesting woman. If it wasn't for your greed you'd have no personality at all. During the evening I noticed something different about you. Not until you came into my room did I realize what it was—you shaved!

The remark that was their beginning now became their farewell.

Sarah didn't collect on Lazarus. Insurance companies do not pay on a body that is missing.

Sarah did marry again. She still has money and more gems, but there is no emerald in her collection.

CHAPTER SIX

Everytime I saw or heard about Lazarus it was a surprise. He was always different. This time he had changed his name to Carol Benson. In his present form he was still young at heart, but his manner of dress made him appear his age. In fact, the mustache, the slight grey at the temples, the horn-rimmed glasses all added years to him. But he didn't have that undernourished complexion that comes to most human beings after age fifty. He had slowed his brisk walk to a nonchalant stroll. Though still a neat dresser, he wasn't as well-groomed as he had been in some of his previous roles. He was living at a hotel in a little town in Ohio, and what he told me, later, about this particular adventure was most touching.

As he described it to me, it was a lovely spring day. The Easter lillies, the lilacs, the variously hued tulips, and the roses, all with healthy, strong stems, splashed the park with a profusion of bright colors. The trees were wearing a bridal veil of pink and white blossoms. A gentle breeze gave a hint of spring, sort of a prologue for those who had to be reminded to have a nice day. Everything was so alive. Children in the park were testing their lungs, yelling and playing all sorts of games. Some were on bikes, dashing out of the way of the well-groomed thoroughbred horses cantering along the bridle path. What a lovely sight to see them prancing and flexing their muscles, their spring coats as shiny as their leather bridles and saddles. It was all a picture of contentment, making it seem as though it's Sunday every day, that the war of Armageddon had been won.

Lazarus was seated on a bench, behind which stood a twenty-five foot bronze statue of a warrior, standing in a chariot, holding a sword high over his head. In the other hand he held the reins taut. The four black horses seemed to be ready to trample down anything that the warrior didn't cut down. Should the statue come to life it was ready to ride roughshod over all living things.

A young lady fell into Lazarus' wandering gaze. It soon became obvious to him that she was in a deep depression. Even so, she was like a lovely flower in a patch of weeds. But she didn't appear to hear or feel the sighing breeze brushing the slender branches of the weeping willow tree, nor did she seem to hear the whippoorwill or the splashing water cascading over the rocks on its way to the little pond. All Lazarus could see was deep anguish on the countenance of the young lady, as she dabbed her tearful eyes with a handkerchief held in her gloved hand. With her other hand she clutched an attache case to her chest. She was not aware that her purse had slid off her lap and fallen to the ground. Lazarus walked over to the bench where the lady was seated, picked up her purse and handed it to her. "You dropped your purse, Miss," he said, tipping his hat with gusto.

"Thank you," she said, not really noticing who she was thanking.

"You can't be too careful in the park, with the purse snatchers in bloom. You know you can walk from one end of the park to the other and never leave the scene of a crime."

She smiled.

"My name is Carol Benson. Do you mind if I sit down?"

"It's all right," she said, putting her handkerchief into her purse and sniffing.

"It looks like you have a little case of hay fever?"

"Just the sniffles."

"You know what is good for the sniffles on a beautiful day like this?"

She looked around her. She hadn't seen the beauty that surrounded her. In fact, it was the first time she really noticed Lazarus.

He was attempting to get comfortable and tried to cross his legs, but the leg slipped off his knee. The girl didn't notice this, but she did study his face, which reminded her of a cheerful cherubim. His eyes sparked, his smile seemed to dance, and he seemed to be filled with adventure. His face was like a magnet that drew a smile to her face.

"You were saying something about the sniffles?"

"Yes," said Lazarus, again trying to cross his leg. But it slipped off the knee again. Quickly, he regained his dignity. "Yes, the best thing for the sniffles is someone you can confide in."

She studied him for a second. Suddenly, she felt she had known him forever. "Have we met before?" she asked, trying to place him.

"If we had, I would have remembered it," he said with authority which he softened with a gentle elegance. He rested both hands on the head of his impressive cane, with its solid gold carving of a lion. He was enjoying the blessings that surrounded him. She, however, was sitting in a slumped position, but when he looked at her she suddenly straightened up.

"That's better," said Lazarus, with a chuckle. "You look a little more ladylike. From the way you were seated, I thought, at first, that you thought yours shoulders were to sit on. Now you look like the loveliness you were born to."

She smiled.

"You are a beautiful young lady. You shouldn't let the weight of the world slump you down like that." Her acceptance of his remarks made him feel free to become more personal. He knew her depression, so common with young folks, was a problem called 'End It All.' "You know," he said, "youth sometimes grows up too fast. They think they have wisdom beyond their years, yet they feel they can't face the truth. They just don't take time to realize that anything worth dying for is worth living for. Dying has never solved one problem. If anyone has found the solution they have kept it a secret because no one has ever returned to explain the answer." He turned to the girl. "I don't mean to be rude, but I don't know your name."

She hesitated a moment, as if doubting the propriety of giving her name to a stranger, but there was something different about him, a kindness and benevolence in his appearance that irresistably compelled her to reply. She extended her hand. "I am Nancy Griffen."

He took her small hand. With her other hand she brushed aside a loose strand of hair from her vision. "Gaylord Griffen is my father. You probably know him. Everybody does."

"No, I can't say that I do." Again, he tried to cross his leg, but it slipped off his knee. Becoming annoyed, Lazarus spoke in a more subdued manner, and he took a deep breath. "Lovely air," he said. "It has a fresher carbon monoxide, not as thick as that stuff you breathe in the downtown district. You know, when I travel I always take a slice of the city air with me so I won't get homesick."

She chuckled and agreed. "The pollution is getting worse." She glanced at the little pond and shook her head.

"That pond is nothing," said Lazarus. "Have you seen the river? It's really polluted! You know, if George Washington were to return, he wouldn't throw a dollar across the Potomac river, he would roll it across." They both seemed to enjoy the remark. "Well, how nice you have cleared up your sniffles."

He looked at her for a second, then said, "You know what is wonderful about life? Without it you are dead." He moved to get a better look at her. "How nice to be able to smile and daydream."

"Do you daydream, Mr. Benson?"

"No. At my age it interferes with my nap." He reached down, picked up his leg and placed it over his knee. But it slowly slid off.

Nancy pretended she didn't notice he was unable to cross

his leg. She did become more responsive to his words. "You know, Mr. Benson, I am glad you came along. You seem special, like you were sent by divine appointment." She brushed a strand of hair from her eyes, then, after thinking for a second, asked, "Are you a minister?"

"Me? No, I couldn't pass the physical."

She laughed. "Then you are a teacher or professor of psychology?"

"I'm that dull, eh?"

"No, no." Again, she nervously pushed the strand of hair from her vision. "You're not a park masher, are you?"

He chuckled. "No, I couldn't pass that physical, either." Again, he crossed his leg and it slid off his knee. So, he stood up and turned his body around, leaving his left leg as a pivot. As he sat down his leg was crossed and in a secure position. He continued his conversation as if what he had just done was normal. "I'm just an old geezer who sticks his nose into other people's concerns. Now your problem . . . I'd say that you are in love."

"Does it show that much?" asked Nancy, with an innocent shyness.

"Be proud of it, let your banner fly high! Love doesn't come to everyone."

"You ever fall in love?"

"No, but I fell in the river once. It's the same thing. You get soaked in both places." Then he became more serious and philosophical. "Love is wonderful. It is the vicissitudes that accompany love that present the real test. But if you can hold your flag high, others may see that you have the strength to carry your standards. If you can't, then you are a lost cause. Even the grim reaper figures you are not worth the take. He says, 'I don't want you if you interfere with a higher authority.'"

She looked at Lazarus. He could sense that she was about to open her heart and thoughts to him. "You know, before you came up," she said, "I was contemplating doing just that."

"Well, if you were it wasn't that obvious. In fact, I wouldn't have noticed you at all if you weren't so pretty. A person who is about to take their life leaves a note or tells someone, hoping they will get attention. You know, the silliest remark I ever heard is someone saying, 'I'll kill myself and you'll be sorry.' What logic! You are dead. What is there to be sorry about? You know, it takes courage to stay alive and face a challenge. Nobody wants anything to do with the other fellow's self-pity. It's such a cowardly way to meet disgrace. Respect for self is the key to dignity, to living. There are no higher principles to which life should be subordinate. Human life is not to be trifled with or played away on a whim." Lazarus became silent. A sudden change came over him. Maybe what he said made him realize, for the first time, that the power to live *was* a special gift. He then looked off into space and continued to speak. "Life is a solemn crisis, even for the most well-adjusted mind. It calls for courage and seriousness of purpose."

As he spoke he became ethereal, almost celestial. What he said touched Nancy. She found him enlightened and articulate. His hands, resting on his cane were steepled, as if he were offering a silent prayer as he spoke.

"Since the beginning of time," he continued, "worthy men and women have admitted their fear of death. Only to the righteous does the thought of death belong. Only they can smile. Seldom do we know the good and the sense of purpose that is within us, and very seldom do we know the good we do for others. So, who knows what is righteous? What gives one the privilege to end a love others have for us? Who are we to take away their only pleasure of giving to that love? Who has the right to take away their happiness? It is a rare case to be forgotten after you are gone. Even after the earth has swallowed you up, even with the passing of time, even after the agony you have caused others, especially those you professed to love, has softened, the hurt you have left is in them forever. They will continue to close their eyes and try to see you, alive and beautiful. If only they could remove that coat of death you wrapped yourself in, that mystical garment that makes you invisible but forever present. They will say, 'Why? She had so much to live for.'

"Let's pretend for a moment you were to plan to invade a power you have no right to, and while you are contemplating ending your precious being, and, though you are not in medical research, for some unknown reason you, and no one else, hear a voice that gives you a cure for cancer. Now, the voice was sent to speak only to you, but you are gone. You see, no one really knows their purpose for being. We do not know our destiny, nor can we alter it. So why disturb something you know nothing about? Best you see life and not let it use you. Leave it to the grim reaper to end it. He will come to you unannounced and everything will be on his terms. He is the one fellow you can't make a deal with."

A puzzled expression came across Nancy's face. Again, she pushed the hair from her eyes as she asked him, "Who is the grim reaper?"

Lazarus thought for a second. "The grim reaper is an artist who takes bodies and souls and sculpts them into dust that blows away in a whirlwind. The only thing that remains is your problem, and the unchanging nature of things good and evil. Kill yourself and all you have done is removed a mask that reveals the genuine character of a coward, who, at best, is remembered as nothing. So why end life before you discover your purpose?

"We are all a mystery. We flit about, not knowing about or giving thought to purpose. Have you ever watched someone who you thought to be a bore? You observe their actions and you do your best not to imitate that person. Well, when that happens they have served a purpose. They taught you to dislike what they do and to make sure you are not like them.

"You didn't ask to be born, so what right do you have to end life? Facing life is that distinction between courage and cowardice. You know, dear," he said as he turned toward Nancy, "if death could solve problems, I would accept the

85

problems of the world, kill myself, and, thereby, end them all.

"It is a short trip from the womb to the tomb. Travel the road with dignity. Along the way you'll meet the great, the small, the good, the bad, Princes and peasants, the renowned and the obscure. You will learn from them, they will learn from you. We are brothers and sisters under the skin, not under the sod."

"You know," said Nancy, "I am really happy we met."

"Thank you," said Lazarus, most proudly.

Then she became tearful again. Lazarus handed her his handkerchief. She dabbed her eyes and blew her nose. Realizing what she had done, she apologized.

"It's O.K.," Lazarus said, "you keep it, I have others." He looked at Nancy for a second. "Do you feel it would help to talk about what is so heartbreaking to you?"

"I am very much in love with a boy named Gerald—Gerald Gilly. He loves me too. We were going to be married, until his father was sent to prison for embezzling funds from my father's construction firm. But Mr. Gilly isn't guilty. I have all the proof right here in this case."

"Sounds rather complicated," said Lazarus as he uncrossed his legs and stretched. "You know, I was thinking," he said, "I'll bet you haven't eaten today?"

"I haven't eaten for two days. I've been so upset."

"Well, you can't run a motor without fuel. Now don't think me rude, but how about you and I going to lunch? There is a lovely restaurant in the park. Let's go have a nice lunch, then, if you feel like talking, I'll listen."

When seen from a distance, the little restaurant in the park took on the charm of a Currier and Ives print. The architectural design echoed that of an old English inn and tavern from the 1700's. Two large carriage lamps flanked the oak doors at the entrance, which was attended by a most impressive doorman, dressed in the costume of a Beefeater and holding a battle axe on a long staff. He was a pleasant fellow, trying to be as stern as the Royal Guard, but his friendly American attitude prevailed.

Lazarus and Nancy arrived at the same moment as two tour buses. The fifty elderly folks getting off the bus and swarming into the building had reservations, so the wait for a table wouldn't be too long.

The inside of the restaurant was attractive, with wood paneling of picklepine on the walls of the high-ceilinged structure. A large oil painting of King George the Fifth and Queen Mary of England hung on the wall. The dining room was rustic, with Elizabethan decor. The tables were covered with white linen tablecloths and napkins, and the place settings were pewter and Sheffield silver. Fresh flower centerpieces added elegance to the tall, silver candle holders. Four harpists rendered Old English Madrigals. In such a setting most guests acquired an aristocratic manner and listened in silent admiration. It would be difficult to imagine a more delightful place to dine.

The hostess was touched by Lazarus and Nancy. She decided, in a moment's glance, that this was a grandfather taking his granddaughter to lunch. She put aside the reservation list, then, with a warm, kindly smile, motioned for them to follow her. She seated them promptly. Lazarus thanked her for the most genial welcome.

Their table faced a leaded glass window, affording them a lovely view of the green lawn and flower beds, which were surrounded by tall pine and weeping willow trees. The cocktail waitress, dressed in Elizabethan costume, was surprised that they both ordered ice tea, so there was no need for a wine list. Soon, another waitress approached the table and announced her name. They both ordered Eggs Benedict.

Lazarus immediately learned many new things about his new acquaintance. She had been at the restaurant many times, including the night of her high school prom. He learned that she had graduated from both high school and college with highest honors, all by the time she was eighteen.

Lazarus didn't delve into her present problem, which remained concealed in the briefcase. He suggested that she would be more comfortable if she placed the case on the chair next to her, but he made no comment as to its obvious importance.

After waiting patiently for about twenty minutes, Lazarus called the hostess to the table and asked, "Did the waitress who took our order leave a large family?" The hostess laughed and promised to rush their order along. He then smiled and said to Nancy, "I guess you give your order and then leave a forwarding address."

Nancy got the giggles, but kept her poise and dignified composure. It would be difficult to convince anyone she had just recently given thought to ending it all because now she seemed self-possessed, ready to meet whatever was in that attache case, not with fear but with courage.

They were finally served. The waitress was apologetic about the bad service. Lazarus smiled. "Think nothing of it, I'm a lousy tipper, anyway."

While they were enjoying their food, a drunk lost his way to the restroom. He wandered into the main dining room area, staggered into a pedestal and pushed over a large potted fern, making a crash that startled the diners. When it splattered all over the floor, the manager hurried to the scene and quickly suggested that the drunk return to his table.

"What's going on?" asked the lush.

"It's all right," assured the manager, without provocation. "But look what you did."

The drunk, trying to focus on the damage, protested, "What do you mean, look what I've done? I didn't do anything!"

It's all right," said the manager, "it was an accident."

The drunk was offended. "But I didn't knock over your tree," he argued. Then he turned to Lazarus. "You were here. Did I knock that tree off the pedestal?"

"No," said Lazarus, "your breath knocked it over."

The sputtering, confused man was taken back to his table by two male waiters while the busboy swept up the mess.

Lazarus and Nancy were served fresh ice tea and, after finishing the food, Lazarus paid the check and they left the restaurant.

Just as they got outside, the manager rushed to them. "You forgot your case," he said as he handed it to Lazarus.

"Thank you," said Lazarus and, then, he turned to Nancy. "Well, it's good to see that the problem in the case has lost its importance."

"Thanks to you," said Nancy, taking her briefcase. Then, she shook his hand. "I am sure glad we met."

"Well, maybe we should do it again. I am frequently in the park right where we met."

Again, she thanked Lazarus for his kindness. She leaned forward and gave him a kiss on the cheek. "Please accept my gratitude. You have made me realize life. I'll give it my love and love everything that belongs to life. You are a nice gentleman. Thanks for the lunch."

"It was a pleasure meeting you. Just don't think about your problem."

"I'll try not to, but it is important. But you have given me a new outlook. It's difficult to imagine that a few hours ago I was thinking of ending it all." Her noble spirit had returned.

"I'll tell you what, I'll give you my phone number. I am at the Windsor Hotel," said Lazarus. "If you feel like talking, well, maybe we can have lunch together again, or we can just talk on the phone."

Nancy said, "Maybe I can figure out what to do about my stepfather."

"Everything will be fine, whatever it is. Just don't leave the living until you get your problem straightened out." They parted.

Lazarus strolled back to his hotel, thinking of the young lady's loveliness, her manners, her gentle thoughts, and her intelligence and sensitivity. She was simple sophistication. He felt that someone special had entered his life and he was sure they would meet again.

A day later the desk clerk called Lazarus' suite to tell him there was a package at the desk, left for him by a young lady. Lazarus had it sent up to his room. It was from Nancy.

With the package was a letter:

Dear Mr. Benson:

First, thank you for the luncheon and the talk. I've been thinking over everything you said. I must tell you my problem. I was hired as a secretary by my stepfather. I was to put some papers in order for him. While doing so, I discovered that he lied at Mr. Gilly's trial. He is guilty of embezzlement, not Mr. Gilly.

Maybe you could go over this evidence and tell me what I should do. I feel I can trust you to hold these books for me after you read the reports.

If you feel I am placing a burden on you, just say so and I will understand.

Love,
Nancy Griffen

P.S. I haven't heard from the grim reaper. In fact, I don't ever care to meet him.

Lazarus held the letter and smiled. His thoughts savored this lovely young lady.

Later, Lazarus went over the books. The next day he received a phone call from Nancy, and they made a date to have lunch again at the little restaurant in the park.

Lazarus was waiting for Nancy when she arrived. What a bit of loveliness she was! She wore a white hat with a yellow ribbon, a yellow bolero jacket trimmed in white, a pleated, full skirt, and white shoes. She was a picture of future happiness, not only externally, but more importantly, internally. It was as if she had not only cleansed her heart, but had also washed her hands in the innocence of discipline. She extended her hand to Lazarus. "It's so nice to see you again, Mr. Benson."

90

Lazarus handed her a lovely little corsage and a small gift-wrapped box. They went to the table he had reserved. After they ordered, Nancy opened her gift, a beautiful silver vase. It was an expensive antique—hallmark, Faberge, 1859. Nancy looked at the flowers and read the inscription on the silver vase: 'To Nancy, my lovely, young friend.' She held the gifts close to her. "That is beautiful. I shall cherish it always."

"Oh, I almost forgot. Here is your briefcase. Everything is in order."

"You are most kind. If only my mother's husband was this understanding."

"You mean your father?" asked Lazarus.

"No," said Nancy, "he is not my father. You see, my mother was pregnant with me for three months when my father, his name was Townsen, was killed in the army in Italy. Mr. Griffen married my mother before I was born. My mother thought it would be better if I thought Mr. Griffen was my father. But soon she realized that he had only married her for her money. She helped him get started in the construction business, then mother realized he was using her. You see, Mr. Benson, Mr. Griffen is not a nice man, he is cruel and unnatural. He gives me great pain. On top of everything, he has destroyed my own happiness and a future life with Gerald because of his dishonesty. Mr. Griffen has ruined Mr. Gilly's life. I have no affection or sympathy for Mr. Griffen. He has consigned my mother to a life of misery. So my decision is unalterable. Each second I think of what he has done strengthens my resolution, and your kind understanding has helped convince me that I am doing the right thing in making his guilt known."

Lazarus was impressed that she was confiding in him on their second meeting. But he had never been one to hastily judge; he required full evidence before deciding to condemn.

At that moment he was thinking that there was nothing to compare to Nancy's natural beauty. Suddenly, it came like a flash. He realized he had seen her lovely face hundreds of times: she was that vision he saw everytime he returned to life. He then saw the picture of his mother over the crib. For a second he felt himself trembling. There, before him, the likeness of the lady—that invisible loveliness he had searched for. At last he had found it, but fifty years too late.

For there is no passion in the tranquil season of life; best to let his heart be wounded by dignity, rather than be agitated by violent emotions. He was too old for indignation. He knew morality without devotion is both defective and unstable. There was no self-pity, for pity is an invention unknown to reason. It cannot regenerate the heart of another person or form the heart to love.

He was in love as a friend, and was not about to allow some corrupting ingredient to enter their relationship, for then, the dearness of trust would pass away like a thunderstorm and corrupt her mind and render deficient what had been a rewarding deed. He had actually saved this lady from even thinking about ending her life. Now he was set on bringing her and her real love together.

After a few seconds, Nancy broke the silence. "Is there something wrong, Mr. Benson?"

"No, everything is fine. I was just wondering what you hear from your young man?"

"I am glad you asked," replied Nancy. "Now, I know it is presumptious on my part, but see that young man standing over there, under the tree?"

Lazarus turned his chair and looked out the window. "What about him?"

"Well, I told him I would ask if you would like to meet him. That's Gerald. You are a good judge of character, I want your opinion of him."

"Well," said Lazarus, folding his napkin and standing up, "I can't tell much about him while he stands over there. I'll go and get him."

"No, no, you stay here. I'll go and fetch him."

"No, dear, dogs fetch! Besides, it is not ladylike for you to go. He should see you in this setting. Always let a gentleman see how alluring you are."

Lazarus hurried to the young man. Nancy watched them shake hands. They both seemed happy as they returned to the table. As they sat down, an elderly lady, seated next to their table, said to Lazarus, "I don't mean to be rude but it's nice to see that you are not some old man out with a young girl."

"Oh, perish the thought!" said Lazarus. "This is my wife and, Gerald, here, is our son. You see, I married her when she was fourteen." The lady sat back in disbelief. "I felt sorry for her," Lazarus continued. "Her first husband was a louse." The elderly lady didn't look at Lazarus again during lunch. Nancy chuckled and Gerald didn't know what to make of Mr. Benson.

"Well," said Lazarus, "you sure have a lovely lady, and I am sure everything will work out. By the way, how is your father? You *are* keeping his spirits in good order?"

"I think so," replied Gerald as he took Nancy's hand.

"Now, I am not the most intelligent man in the world," said Lazarus, "but I have an idea how we can clear up this whole mess. I went to the newspaper and read about your father's trial. We don't have to go over that ordeal, but I want to hear your thinking about what I have in mind."

"I am eager to hear what you have to say," said Gerald. "Nancy thinks you are the kindest man she has ever met."

"Well," said Lazarus, "that's only because she hasn't given you a chance to prove yourself." He gave Gerald a pat on the arm.

"I told you what a gentleman he is," said Nancy, giving Gerald's hand a squeeze.

"Well, I was getting a little jealous of you," replied Gerald.

"Gerald," said Lazarus, in a fatherly tone, "never be jealous, for it is a mistrust. If you don't trust someone, then you are not in love, for love is trust. Now, so only we know what

I propose to do." He reached into his inside coat pocket and brought out a letter.

At that moment the waitress stepped up to the table. "Are you ready to order?" she asked. Gerald ordered lunch. After the waitress left the table, Lazarus handed the letter to Nancy.

"Now scoot closer together so both of you read this at the same time. If there is anything that should not be said, just tell me. If it seems all wrong and you would rather handle it in some other fashion, there will be no hard feelings. It's just an idea that might work. The letter is intended for Mr. Griffen."

They both read the letter:

Mr. Griffen:

After meeting your lovely daughter, I discovered she has a wonderful idea that you'll clear up a most heart-breaking injustice that has been dealt not only to you and your family, but even more so to your friend, Mr. Gilly. Here is, I believe, a workable plan that will clear everyone's name.

You, Mr. Griffen, will go to the District Attorney and explain to him that you are preparing for a audit and, a few weeks ago, your daughter was hired by your company to put your books in order. As she did, she discovered a discrepancy that has all but destroyed your reputation, not to mention that of Mr. Gilly, an honorable man. I find that before selling shares in the Winter View properties, it was suggested that "we sell stock in our company," not just as an investment in the Winter View properties. There were but fifty shares sold in the first project and a hundred in future projects. But in the hassle of strikes and building delays, this proposal was put aside and was never brought up at any board meeting again.

Now I discover that Mr. Gilly was sentenced to prison for something we were all negligent about.

94

There has been no embezzlement, nor was anyone swindled—all the monies are intact.

I suggest we have a grand jury hear the mistake, free Mr. Gilly and restore his good name, for each person who invested is fully covered and will have shares in future titles. In going over the accounting I realized this was our original plan and, also, discovered the injustice that has been done out of negligence on all our parts. This should be rectified as soon as possible for the sake of an innocent man and his reputation, as well as the reputation of the company. The company should assume all costs incurred in resolving this matter. I am certain all of this can be clarified behind closed doors.

Sincerely,
A Shareholder

Nancy asked, "Do you think the district attorney will understand?"

Lazarus spoke in a low voice. "Well, look at it this way. There is an election coming up. If the D.A. wants to prove he is a just man then he can pursue this and point out that even big business can make a mistake."

"What if Mr. Griffen won't go for it?" asked Gerald.

"If he is that stubborn and is all that dishonest, you have a set of books. Let your conscience take over. If he has any self-respect and any love for Nancy and her mother, I have no doubt that he will do it. Now, I will call Mr. Griffen and tell him his daughter is seeing an older man. I am sure he'll pay a visit to the hotel."

"Won't he recognize your voice if he does come?"

"I have a small container of helium gas from which I'll inhale. That will change my voice on the phone."

Lunch was served and no more was said. After lunch, Lazarus paid the check. As they walked out of the restaurant, Lazarus stopped and said to the maitre d', "There is something I have wanted to do." He walked to the fireplace. On it was a ceramic dog. On the table nearby was a ceramic cat which he picked up and placed next to the dog, and said, "Sic 'em!" Then he walked out of the restaurant.

Lazarus escorted Nancy back to her car. Young Gerald drove off in his, after thanking Lazarus for his help. Nancy was most affectionate with her good bye, kissing Lazarus on the cheek and hugging his neck. Then she got into her car and drove off.

"I'll be at the hotel by six," shouted Lazarus as he tipped his hat to the two ladies who had been seated next to him in the restaurant. As he walked by their car, he smiled and said, "I guess it is hard to hear everything that was said. Have you ever thought about getting a hearing aid?"

"You know," one of them said to the other, "that old reprobate is using that young man to cover his actions."

"Well, you know who the girl is, don't you?"

"I've seen her before. Why, that's Gaylord Griffen's daughter. I think Mr. Griffen should be told."

"It's none of my business," said the old bitty's friend.

"Well, I didn't like the smart answer he embarrassed me with. I think I'll give Mr. Griffen a call. It's disgusting, a young girl like that with such an old man. It is obvious he has swept her off her feet with his big shot manners."

A call was made by the little old lady and Griffen suddenly became fatherly.

Mildred also received a call from the busy body, so she told Gaylord about Nancy seeing an elderly man. Mr. Griffen called his friend, the chief of police, and they paid a visit to Lazarus at his hotel. Their intention was to throw a scare into him and warn him to stay away from Nancy.

CHAPTER SEVEN

It was late afternoon when a knock came at the door of Lazarus' hotel suite, which consisted of two rooms, furnished most expensively in light, cheerful colors. Lazarus, seated at the desk in the large sitting room when the knock came, got up, went to the door, looked through the peek hole, then opened it. Standing in the hall were Mr. and Mrs. Griffen, with a heavy-set chief of police, named Williger. After they introduced themselves, Lazarus invited them in. He knew they had a problem because they looked conspiratorial.

Lazarus was most polite. "Had you let me know you were coming I would have ordered some refreshments," he said in his most cordial manner.

But the chief of police replied abruptly. "We won't be here long, and you have twenty-four hours to get out of town!"

Lazarus looked at the officer in disbelief. "You sound like an old cowboy movie. Although, you should have added, 'This town ain't big enough for both of us!' " Then, after closer scrutiny of the fat officer, he added, "In fact, if you put on more weight there won't be room enough for anybody." Lazarus sat down and turned to Mrs. Griffen. "Well," he said, "at last we meet. Won't you be seated? Nancy had planned for us to have lunch tomorrow. You have a nice daughter, Mrs. Griffen."

Mr. Griffen removed a cigar from his lips. His voice was loud and authoritative. "We are here to see that she stays that way."

"You see," broke in the buggy officer, "we don't take it lightly when an old man tries to force himself on a young lady."

Lazarus took on a surprised, shocked expression. "Good

heavens, you mean like the police officers who stake out a spot up at Lovers' Lane, then molest young girls who are with their boyfriends? While one officer roughs up the young man, the other police officer crawls into the back seat and tells the young girl it's the only way to prevent arrest."

The officer began to stutter and stammer. "Where did you hear a thing like that?"

Lazarus smiled. "You know that blind man who sells newspapers on the corner of Fifth and Main? Well, he is the only one in town who hasn't mentioned it."

"Well, I'll put a stop to that."

"You should," retorted Lazarus. "You are getting a little too fat for the back seats of cars." Lazarus turned to Mrs. Griffen and asked, "Can I get you something, Mrs. Griffen?"

"No, Mr. Benson, I am fine."

"You are more than fine. In fact, you are more lovely than Nancy had described you."

Mrs. Griffen was taken by his charm, and felt that what he said weren't just flattering words. "Thank you," she said.

"I am sorry that you have the wrong impression of me," said Lazarus.

"We have a real good idea about you." The Chief again stumbled over his words.

"Now you listen to me," Lazarus continued, emphasizing each word. "This visit is obviously premeditated, therefore what you're saying is not an accidental untruth." Turning to the officer, he moved and spoke most forcefully. "Now, you fat jackass! Which *is* a fact! Either you act like an officer and a gentleman or I will spend every dime I have to get you expelled from office." He reached in his pocket and brought forth a paper. "Here is a letter of credit for two million dollars." (It was a phoney letter, but at that point who checks?) "I'll spend even more to see you are put out to pasture."

The officer calmed down.

"Now that I understand this is not a social call but an invasion, maybe you should state just exactly why you are here."

The chief mustered some courage, pointed his finger in Lazarus' face and yelled in a most defiant tone, "I want you out of town in twenty-four hours!"

Lazarus gave him a deadly stare and then pointed his finger at the chief. "And I want you out of this room in one minute or I'll sue you for invasion of privacy, slander, and a few other things. And before you leave, I remind you, sir, of your oath of office. 'Jus natural est quod apud homines eandem habit potentiam.' Which, translated from Latin, means 'Natural right is that which has the same force among all mankind.'"

Not one person in the room understood what Lazarus had just said and he didn't know why he had said it.

Mr. Griffen took over. "Look, Fred," he said to the chief, "wait outside. If I need you, I'll call."

The chief walked to the door and said to Lazarus, "I'll see you in hell."

"Yes, I'm sure we will meet again," said Lazarus

As the officer exited he slammed the door.

Lazarus turned and extended his hand to Mrs. Griffen. "Can I get you some refreshments? There is a bottle of sherry in the refrigerator."

"No thank you."

Turning to Mr. Griffen, he said, "Please sit down. May I get you something, Mr. Griffen?"

"You can call me Gaylord. I will have a slug of that wine." Griffen became more agreeable. "I'll come to the point," he said as he flopped into the chair. "What's between you and my daughter?"

"There is never anything between friendship but its solid force."

"Don't you think you are a little old to be seeing a girl of eighteen?"

Lazarus was pouring a drink for Mr. Griffen. "What has age got to do with seeing someone older than the other person?

Santa Claus is over four hundred years old and he sees children aged two to twelve who tell him secrets their mothers and fathers are not aware of." Lazarus directed his remarks to Mrs. Griffen as he handed Gaylord the glass of wine. "You know, Mrs. . . . May I call you Mildred?"

"Please do," she responded affably.

"You are truly a gallant woman. You see, I know quite a bit about you, and I will not repeat all the praise from your lovely daughter. You should be grateful that she met me before another scandal like Mr. Griffen's embezzlement and casting of the blame on Mr. Gilly. I am sure a suicide in the family would only add to the gossip."

"A suicide?" repeated Mrs. Griffen, in disbelief.

"It's O.K. There is no danger now," Lazarus assured her.

"What gossip?" asked Mr. Griffen.

"I have a report on my desk that tells how you sold one hundred and fifty per cent of the shares in a building project when there were only fifty which were legally saleable."

"Gaylord, what is he saying?" asked Mildred.

Griffen became sheepish. "I haven't the slightest idea," he lied.

"It's all in his handwriting. You see, Mildred," said Lazarus, "it is called 'swindle' when subscription investment shares are oversold. What happened is that he let Mr. Gilly sign maybe two hundred certificates. Mr. Gilly offered his name to a written contract for capital stock to limited partners, but your husband oversold. Mr. Gilly was unaware of this because the monies were taken by your husband. Naturally, if there is a discrepancy noticed, Mr. Gilly is responsible because he was in charge of sales. Mr. Gilly knew about the fifty subscribed stocks, not the other one hundred and fifty at fifty thousand cash for each share.

"You see, your husband built a project in a neighborhood that he figured would not sell. So, if the money was lost no one would be the wiser. Just write it off as a bad investment.

100

Unfortunately, for Mr. Gilly, it did sell, and the stockholders wanted their dividends. There is nothing like greed to attract greed, so when the stockholders wanted their money, the only thing Mr. Griffen could do was cast all guilt on Mr. Gilly.

"Now, Nancy intends to go to court and get her boyfriend's father released from prison. But there is a way out for you, Gaylord. A new trial, but you must ask for it, not Nancy."

"I'll have another glass of wine," said Mr. Griffen.

Lazarus looked at him. "Not while we talk business. You see, your husband not only juggled the books, he has also swindled your money."

"Now wait a minute! What you are saying is libel!" shouted Mr. Griffen.

"It is *liable* to get you sent up for perjury, misappropriation of funds, plus a little double entry with the IRS. You see, on my desk is a second set of your books. Not those produced in court, but the ones you had hidden in your safe."

"That's a lie!" shouted Mr. Griffen.

"There is no need to shout. You are safe. You should be glad I came along, for I have saved you from several tragedies. First, I talked your daughter out of committing suicide. Secondly, I plan to keep you from going to jail, even while we are freeing Mr. Gilly. Third, what the chief is doing to you is called 'blackmail,' but you can get rid of him when you demand a new trial for Mr. Gilly."

"You are insane," sputtered Mr. Griffen.

"No. You are, if you don't listen. All you have to do is ask for a hearing with a grand jury. You explain to the District Attorney that a few weeks ago you hired your daughter to put your books in order, that you feel there has been a injustice done an innocent man, that before you built Winter View properties you came up with other properties to be built, that the stockholders didn't buy into shares but into your whole company, not just Winter View. Well, with strikes and union problems the idea for limited partners got lost in the shuffle

101

and that all efforts and thoughts went toward getting the Winter View project finished. But the money is in safe keeping and the extra shares were sold to the holders of share certificates as shares which they could exchange, making them limited partners in the company. Explain that there is readily no discrepancy, only a mix-up when the original idea was pushed aside and forgotten. Had not your daughter discovered the minutes of the meeting, this innocent man would serve years in jail for something he did not do.

"If you don't do it this way, then the real truth will come out. For all I have to do is encourage Nancy to go ahead with her original plan and take you to court, and I will pay for the lawyers to free Mr. Gilly, just so Nancy can marry her young man."

Mr. Griffen became interested. "You would do that for Nancy?"

"For a price."

"What kind of price?"

"Adding up the amount you took in, I'd say I would need that much to return these books to your hands and to get that blackmailing pious blimp with the corroded badge off your back. Then, I would take his advice and leave town and never contact Nancy again. But a quick exit from this city would be expensive."

"How much?"

"I'd say about two hundred thousand dollars."

"Obviously, I don't carry that much money around, and a check for that much would arouse suspicion."

"And you could put a stop payment, once you have the books."

Griffen looked at Mildred's finger. "Give me your ring."

"What for?" asked Mildred, covering the ring as if to protect it.

"It's worth over two hundred thousand, that's what for!" shouted Mr. Griffen.

"No!" said Mildred. "You have used me for the last time."

Griffen winked at her. "It's only a loan, I'll get you a better ring."

Not knowing exactly why he winked, she, nevertheless, removed the ring and handed it to Gaylord.

"Here," he said. "See for yourself, it's a perfect stone."

Lazarus took it to the light. Griffen stood behind him, then raised his walking stick and brought it down on Lazarus' head. Though he wasn't really hurt by the blow, Lazarus dropped to the floor, slipping the ring into his pocket as he fell. Then he went into his trance.

Griffen grabbed the books from the desk, then ran to the door and motioned for the chief to come in from the hall. "Come in here and take care of that creep," he instructed the chief, pointing to Lazarus.

The chief walked over and kneeled down beside Lazarus. "What happened?"

Griffen shouted, "Never mind, I have the books. Let's get out of here!"

Mildred was looking for the ring. "My ring! Open his hand, he has my ring."

"Don't worry about it, he's not going anywhere with it," said the officer as he opened Lazarus hand. "There's no ring in his hand. What happened?"

"I hit him with my walking stick."

Mildred kept looking all around the room. "He must have dropped it." She was on the verge of panic.

The chief said, "You know, I think you hit him a little hard. He's dead."

Griffen just stood, dumbfounded. "He couldn't be, I didn't hit him that hard."

"Well, he is dead!"

"Oh my God!" sobbed Mildred.

"You both get out of here. I'll handle this," said the chief.

"Oh dear, what are we going to do?" asked Mildred, now a nervous wreck.

The chief became his old repulsive self as he examined Lazarus again. "Yeah, he's dead." He looked at Mrs. Griffen. "Look, Mildred, there is no need for you to get mixed up in this."

She turned to her husband. "What are we going to do? You've killed a man!"

"I'll tell you what you are going to do," commanded the chief. "You are going to get out of here. The guy is dead." He then looked at Griffen and shook his head. "Help me get him out of here." He noticed that Lazarus had already packed his bags, so he said to Griffen, "We will take these, then it looks like he checked out."

"I can't do that. Where are you going to take him?" asked Griffen, staring at the body.

"Out the back elevator," said the chief. "You help me get him into my car. I'll do the rest."

"What if someone sees us?"

"We will tell them he's drunk."

"What about my ring?" Mildred asked.

"I'll have one of my men check the room later. Right now you, Mildred, go home!"

The two men carried the limp body down the hall to the garage. The chief went to get the police car. Griffen leaned against Lazarus to hold him up while they waited. Then they put the body in the back seat of the police car.

"You go home and don't worry," the chief told Griffen. Then he got in the car and drove down the alley. When he got to the street he turned on to the main drag, then drove out to the edge of town to a deserted road. There he stopped the car and dragged the body into the bushes, where he left Lazarus with his suitcases. Then he drove away.

A sewer drainage ditch, filled with rocks, thistles, and shrub oak, trimmed with poison ivy, isn't exactly the sort of exotic foliage anyone would likely choose as a final resting place.

Lazarus lay in the ditch for over an hour. He slowly became aware of something that wasn't a routine part of his return to life. It was the first time he felt a sense of isolation. He particularly noticed that it had taken him a longer time to revive; he was in a weakened condition. His clothing was wet with perspiration, and his body was chilled. Through the tears that blurred his vision, he tried to control his twitching fingers. He stared at his hands, which shook as if they were holding a vibrator. He realized that he had come closer to the fringe of death than ever before. He couldn't shrug off the feeling, it was too nightmarish. His knees were weak, his heart was twisted with anguish. Never had he felt so alone.

Again, he closed his eyes and relived his return. He saw not the original vision of his mother, but now Nancy and his mother were perceived as one. They stood before him with sad expressions, tears cascading over their pale cheeks. It was then that Lazarus realized that Nancy *was* the likeness of his mother.

He now realized that life was more than a challenge to be met. He now knew that love was life's foundation and that honesty to that love was the meaning of life. Nancy became very special to him. There were no passionate desires, no complexities, nothing brash or ostentatious. There was just a true friendship.

Perhaps as an omen, he was immediately reminded that he had cheated on a trust by taking Nancy's mother ring. Quickly, he searched his pockets, hoping that the chief hadn't found it. It was there! Holding the ring to his fist, he brought it to his lips and whispered, "I am so ashamed. I must return the ring. I must return the ring."

As he got himself together and picked up the suitcases, he wondered how he could return the ring without arousing the suspicion of Griffen and the chief. If they learned he was alive, not only would he be in danger, but Nancy's chances of helping free Mr. Gilly from prison would be gone. His head was spinning. Logic wouldn't jell. Like a feather in the wind, he moved to and fro, mumbling a prayer that was a combination of asking for forgiveness and revenge. He felt terribly incompetent, but this only made him more determined to help Nancy.

More and more, he realized he was dealing with those who made the world a sick place, and their poison had no antidote. (Lazarus was no saint, but he would never run last in the human race. Where emotions are concerned, he could have revolutionized honesty.)

After finally regaining his dignity and composure, he scrambled up the banks of the ditch, dragging his suitcases along. After a struggle he made his way to the main highway some half a mile away. He hoped to hitch a ride to the nearest telephone and call Nancy. His exhaustion made the walk to the highway seem endless.

He stood along the side of the freeway and cars sped by as though he were invisible. Finally, along came a Good Samaritan. He was a jolly, little farmer with a sunburned red nose who was driving a truck loaded with empty chicken crates. As the old truck came to a stop in front of Lazarus, the farmer asked him, "How far ya goin'?"

"Just to the nearest phone," answered Lazarus.

"Well, throw yer bags in the back and git in. There's a gas station jest down the road."

"I sure thank you for the lift," said Lazarus, trying to get comfortable.

"Glad ta help," said the happy, little man. "People don't pick up hitchhikers much anymore." The farmer looked at Lazarus several times, then asked, "Are ya all right? Ya look like ya been rentin' yerself out as a speed bump."

Lazarus laughed. "I'm fine. Just tired."

"Well, I never saw anyone so tired that they bled. Ya sure yer all right?"

"Yes, I'm fine. I just want to get to a phone and call my friends to come and get me."

"Ya didn't git beat up, did ya? Ya look like round fifteen of a dirty fight."

"No, I stumbled and fell down back there." To distract attention from himself, Lazarus said, "Nice truck you have."

"It's old," said the farmer, with a chuckle. "Ahm thinkin'

about gittin' a new truck. This one's so old its got Roman numerals. And the cost of repairs! Those guys let ya know what's meant by highway robbery. Last week I took my car in fer four new shocks—and I got five." He glanced at Lazarus to see if he got the joke. "I couldn't believe the bill. The lowest number on it was the phone number."

Lazarus smiled, which encouraged the highway comic to go on.

"I call this truck 'flattery' cause it gits you nowhere. But it's a nice old truck, fer all that. Ya know, they made 'em better in the old days. A friend of mine buys a little car, hears a knockin', raises the hood and finds a jap still working on the motor. American cars are good, but I saw where they called back fifty thousand new ones 'cause they'd put somethin' on 'em that would last a lifetime."

Lazarus was glad when he saw the gas station ahead. The truck stopped. Lazarus thanked the little man, got out and headed for the public phone booth. He took out a little notebook, found a number and dialed Gerald Gilly's home. "Hello," he said, "I'd like to speak with Gerald Gilly."

"Speaking."

"Gerald, this is Carol Benson. I'm calling from a gas station. Yes, I'm fine, but can you pick up Nancy and come out and get me? It is imperative that I talk to both of you. I am at the gas station on the Jefferson Road turn off on Route Fifty. I'll wait right here, but hurry. I'll tell you what happened when you get here. Don't tell anyone but Nancy where you are going."

While waiting for Nancy and Gerald, Lazarus went to the restroom to wash the blood from the scratches on his face, hoping to make himself look more presentable. He put on a fresh shirt and tie. Thirty minutes later the young pair arrived. He greeted them as they pulled into the gas station.

Nancy became very concerned when she saw him. "Good heavens!" she cried, "what happened to you? Shall we take you to the hospital?"

"No, no, I'm all right," Lazarus assured her.

"Your voice, what happened to your voice?"

"An after effect of dehydration. I am fine. Let's go somewhere where we can talk."

Nancy was persistent. "Please tell me what happened to you. What are you doing out here?" She helped him into the car. Gerald put his bags in the back seat. They drove out of the station, drove a short ways down the road and parked under a street lamp. "Now," said Nancy, "'what happened?"

Lazarus took a deep breath, then said, "Mr. Griffen and the Chief of Police tried to kill me."

Nancy and Gerald were stunned. "I can't believe it," said Nancy.

"It's true. This afternoon, your mother, Mr. Griffen, and the chief came to my room at the hotel. At first, I thought you had talked to Mr. Griffen because they ordered me out of town."

"My mother did that!"

"No, no dear, your mother is a lovely lady, but Griffen and that police chief are like something you'd find under a wet rock. Anyway, the chief ordered me out of town. I became angry and ordered him out of my room. They were under the impression that I was some kind of freak who was out seducing young girls. You, being the particular young girl."

"The filthy degenerate!" exclaimed Nancy.

"What happened then?" asked Gerald.

"Well, I let them know I was aware of the reason your father was in prison and that I had proof Griffen was an embezzler. But I explained there was a way of clearing all the names involved and that I had a copy of his secret bookkeeping. Then I did something I'm ashamed of. I told him the book would cost him. It's a good thing I gave the books back to you or Mr. Gilly would be in prison a long time. Anyway, Griffen then offered your mother's ring as payment."

"Oh, no, that's the only security she has left!"

"Don't worry about it. She was reluctant, but Griffen gave her a wink. She gave up the ring and Griffen promised her a replacement. He handed me the ring. While I was looking at the diamond, he sneeked up behind me and hit me over the head. As I fell to the floor I slipped the ring into my pocket." Lazarus reached into his pocket and handed the ring to Nancy. "Here is your mother's ring. But don't give it to her yet. If you do they will know something is wrong. At the right time you may give the ring back to your mother—maybe when she gets wise and leaves Griffen."

"What happened when Griffen hit you over the head?" wondered Gerald.

"I remained still. The chief examined me and pronounced me dead. But he told them not to worry, he would take care of the body. They made your mother leave. She was most concerned. Then Griffen and the chief dragged me to the freight elevator, took me to the garage and put me in the squad car. The chief drove me to a deserted road and threw me in a ditch."

Nancy held his hand. "Oh, you poor thing," she said tearfully, while gently stroking his face.

"Don't cry, dear. I am fine as long as they believe I am dead. But we must use great strategy."

"I wonder why they believed you to be dead?" asked Nancy.

"I'll explain that to you later. Now, what is the next big town around here, one that has stores and a hotel?"

"Ashland is about six miles from here," suggested Gerald.

"Then, let's go to Ashland. Right now, I have to pull my wits together."

They arrived in Ashland and Lazarus checked into the hotel, paid the rent for three days and signed in under the name of Jim Benson. Turning to Nancy, he said, "I am now Carol's brother, James."

When they got to the room, Lazarus opened his suitcase and unzipped a secret compartment from which he took a scrapbook of his theatrical days. He handed her the publicity and stories about The Great Lazarus. "Here," he said, "while I shower and freshen up a bit I want you both to read through this scrapbook, so you can get better acquainted with me. I think you will understand why they believed me dead."

In ten minutes Lazarus returned to the room. Nancy stood looking at him for a moment, then leaned forward and kissed him on the cheek. Lazarus turned to Gerald and said, "You see what happens when you reach my age? They can't find your lips anymore."

They all laughed.

Nancy's eyes welled up. "Now I know why you were sent to help me. You are like an angel. I am so sorry I was responsible for getting you hurt. I am sorry I got you mixed up in my problems."

"You didn't. It's now our problem."

"What can I do to thank you?" asked Nancy, dabbing her eyes.

"First, you must promise that you will never reveal what you have read in that scrapbook."

Nancy looked into his eyes. "Now I know why you know so much about death."

"Just enough to avoid it as long as I can." His eyes were tearful, his voice had a sob. "Now both of you listen to me. First, your mother's ring. When you see her, notice that it's not on her finger, mention it in front of Griffen. He promised to get her a better ring. Keep at it until he does. As far as they know, I am dead. When there is nothing mentioned in the news, they will wonder what happened to the body. I am sure the chief will drive out to the ditch and check it. This will add to the mystery.

"Now, tomorrow I will start my disguise. In three days I will be fully recovered from a few bruises and will meet you at the Windsor Hotel at eleven o'clock in the morning."

Gerald kept staring at Lazarus. "Can you really die and come back?"

Lazarus shook his head. "Just forget everything I told you.

If you, in any way, bring up the subject, your father is going to rot in prison."

"I promise," said Gerald. "I am sorry, but I just can't believe anyone could die and come back."

"Forget it. Don't even mention it to each other. Now both of you go home. I hope you won't recognize me when we meet again, but I'll let you know it's me. I will go to the Windsor Hotel and check in as Carol's brother, gather his belongings and pay his bill. Then I will contact the chief and Mr. Griffen.

"Now comes the part you will play in this little diabolical plot. It will be a game of suggestions and subliminal phrases. You are responsible for creating a very serious climate. First, you must show great concern about your missing friend, Mr. Benson. This will cause great anxiety and confusion in Mr. Griffen's already muddled mind. You make it known that you are going to ask for an investigation into Mr. Benson's whereabouts, that you have a psychic feeling that he has been murdered because he was going to help get Mr. Gilly out of prison. To sidetrack any murder investigation both Griffen and the chief will put pressure on the district attorney to open a trial, using what I have suggested in my plan." He stopped and shook his head. "I should say, Carol's plan. You see how easy it is to slip up. So we must keep a clear head at all times.

"Nancy, you and Gerald go to the D.A.'s office and plant in his mind that getting Mr. Gilly released from prison will help him get reelected to office because the people will see him as a man of fairness and justice. Keep planting the word 'murder' in Griffen's and the chief's minds until the trial, then slowly let your concern about Mr. Benson diminish.

"You have three days, and I will take over. Above all, do not let threats or suggestions muddle your minds. Above all, don't allow emotions or sentiments to rule your heart. I am sure you can give understanding to your dear mother, but remember to use the word 'murder' whenever Mr. Benson's name is mentioned around the two gentlemen. The word will

111

gradually unnerve them. Eventually, Mr. Griffen will be glad to escape from the prison he has now put himself in, for he has imprisoned his soul and this is what will finally get Mr. Gilly released from prison."

Nancy was fascinated with his solution. "I wish I had teachers like you in college."

"You would have only learned from the book. What has happened to you has made you realize that real life is not explained in books, only in your heart. Books try to teach discipline. Now you can make use of that discipline by living."

"Will you be all right?" asked Nancy.

"I will be fine. Thank you both for coming to my rescue."

"I still say you were sent to us by special appointment," said Nancy, trying to express her gratitude.

Lazarus was pleased and said, "You don't realize how special you are to me. Now, you two run along. Remember what to remember and what to forget."

They said good night and left Lazarus alone.

Exhausted, he lay down on the bed and went to sleep. When he awoke he called the Windsor Hotel and left a message for Carol Benson that his brother had called. The hotel would receive ten such calls in the next three days.

Lazarus accomplished a lot in those days. Each time he called the Windsor and was told that no one answered in Carol Benson's room, he left a message that his brother Jim Benson had called. As his scratches and bruises healed he went shopping for a wardrobe, buying both new and old things. The suit he bought off the rack reminded him of his leaner days. The suit he purchased from the rummage store was part of the paraphernalia needed for his new character, Jim Benson, brother of the late Carol Benson. A second-hand suitcase would denote extensive travel. The gold pocket watch added a little of the old-fashioned touch of a Victorian dandy. He had calling cards printed which announced that he was Dr. James Benson, criminologist. Each article served a purpose and would assist him in his little drama of revenge. He was about to teach rank amateurs that one cannot be inexperienced when practicing the art of hoodwinking. He also knew that the most minute detail must become a new habit, for cleverness can sometimes lead to defeat. It is easy to make noticeable mistakes. He rehearsed and perfected every move so that his newly acquired limp would not betray him. He bought two pairs of the same shoes, one a half size too small. This helped to give him a natural limp because a faked limp can easily give you away, especially in an argument or panic situation when the faker forgets to limp. Lazarus knew he must not be caught off guard.

He studied his characterization so that nothing could be identifiable with Carol. His eating habits became as bland as the tasteless food he ate. His sleeping habits changed—a warm-up suit replaced pajamas, even one of his bedroom slippers was a size too small. He could not assume anything, yet he had to be comfortable with each thing he did. A bottle of Dr. Scholl's Freezetone would be part of his medical supply to ease the pain of the corns the tight shoe would develop.

Shaving off his mustache gave him a more youthful appearance and the goldrimmed half glasses and the greenish-blue contact lenses added a more scholarly look. The toupee the hair stylist sold him looked like a glob of hemp that was glued onto his head. The barber assured him it was real hair, but every time he passed a dog he expected the hair to stand straight up. His cane, though a prop, became a third hand and arm. He used the handgrip as a shepherd uses a staff.

All in all, his manner of dress gave him a dauntless, casual, befuddled appearance. He became observant of all things through a kind of rural curiosity. His attitude wasn't without kindness, but chivalry wouldn't be one of his more obvious qualities.

One problem was the tight shoe. It was starting to produce agony already. But it reminded him of his purpose—that was, helping Nancy. But even with her he would be ill-mannered. (The most difficult part of his acting job was pretending that Nancy was meaningless to him.) His voice would be gruff and loud, his words spoken in a monotone. He would be attentive but without brilliant conversational phrases. Instead, he would make each point precisely, positively, and, most often, rudely. In fact, he would be borish prig who smugly adheres to rigid standards and is totally annoying to those around him.

After three days of preparation and rehearsal and a silent prayer that his disguise would be authentic, he packed his bags and hired a cab to take him to the Windsor Hotel.

As he emerged from the cab the doorman at the Windsor offered to assist him with his luggage, but Lazarus became cantankerous and stepped between his bags and the doorman. "Never mind, young man, I'll handle that." He hooked the handgrip of his cane to the suitcase handle and pulled it behind him.

Standing at the entrance of the hotel were Nancy and Gerald. A man moved behind Nancy so casually that he immediately drew Lazarus' attention. As the man reached out and pulled Nancy's handbag from under her arm, then took off in a mad dash toward Lazarus, he unhooked his cane from the bag, reached out with it and hooked the thief around the neck. The man gasped and did a Steve Brody. His feet flew off the ground and he landed flat on his back. Lazarus then held the shaft of the cane with one hand and drew a sword which was attached to the handle. He held the point of the sword to the man's chest.

Nancy ran to Lazarus, who was now giving orders as to what others were to do. Handing the purse to Nancy, he turned to the doorman and yelled, "Don't stand there like an idiot, call the police!"

Two bellboys grabbed the thief.

Lazarus resheathed the sword and walked away, pulling his suitcase behind him with the cane. He looked like an airline hostess.

Nancy, whom he had completely ignored, ran to him. "Thank you for what you did," she said most gratefully.

"Don't thank me, young lady," blurted Lazarus, "but you should be more careful with your things." He then proceeded into the hotel lobby.

Nancy glanced at Gerald in a questioning way. "Do you think it was him?" she asked Gerald, who stood in disbelief after seeing what had just happened.

"Sure didn't act like him."

"Let's find out." They followed him at a distance.

The tight shoe and its newness made the limp authentic. In fact, anyone watching could have felt the pain. Nancy and Gerald followed him to the registration desk. Lazarus continued to affect his gruff, rural style. His manners had been absolutely suitable for the episode with the snatcher, but he knew one wrong move, or the use of any former mannerism, would give him away. So his attitude remained ingenuous. He continued to ignore Nancy and Gerald. At the reservation desk Lazarus was irritable.

"Good afternoon, sir," said the overly polite clerk. "You have a reservation?"

"I think so. My name is James Benson. My brother Carol Benson stays here. I'll register and share his room with him. Could you ring his room and tell him I am here."

The young desk clerk pointed in the direction of the house phone. "You'll find the house phone right over there."

"I don't call houses. Just give me the key to room 1515. And get me the manager. I want to speak with him."

The clerk picked up the phone.

"You don't use the house phone?" asked Lazarus, smugly.

Before she could call, the manager of the hotel walked up.

"This is Mr. Benson," said the clerk as she put the receiver back into its cradle.

The manager extended his hand, which Lazarus barely shook. "We have been expecting you, sir. Thank you for what you did a few minutes ago."

"And there will be a lot more you can expect. I have reason to believe that my brother was murdered in this hotel. What do you have to say to that?"

The manager became anxious and frustrated. "Could we go up to your brother's room and talk?"

Nancy, who had been standing close by, walked up to Lazarus. He gave her a perturbed glance. "Oh, it's you. How many times are you going to thank me?" he asked her, pretending to be very annoyed.

"I am Nancy Griffen."

"I am sure the name comes in handy for you."

"I am Nancy, Carol's friend."

"That's nice." He suddenly changed his attitude. "Oh, that Nancy Griffen." He took her hand and acted pleased. "Carol told me about you, and about that crooked stepfather you got rooked with." He then changed his tone. "Carol is dead, you know."

Nancy gave a stunned response. "Oh, no! What happened?"

"He was murdered. You come up to the room and I'll tell you about it." He then looked at Gerald. "Is this young man with you?"

"Yes," said Gerald, "I am Gerald Gilly. Remember?"

"I don't think we have met."

"I am sure Carol told you about Gerald's father," said Nancy. "His father is the gentleman in prison."

"Oh well, we'll talk up in the room," said Lazarus.

The manager suggested that Lazarus keep his voice down. "You know, sir, everyone in the lobby can hear every word you say."

"Naturally," said Lazarus, "my enunciation is perfect."

"Right this way," said the manager, adopting a forced smile.

"I have other business at the desk," said Lazarus. He walked to the clerk and handed her a key to a safety deposit box. "I'd like the box," he told her. "And I'd like to pay for my lodging in advance."

116

The girl reached into a file and brought out a card. "This says, 'Mr. Carol Benson or Mr. James Benson.'"

"That's right, I am *or*," said Lazarus.

"Sign here, sir," she said, handing him a ballpoint pen and pushing the card toward him. Lazarus signed the card. Meanwhile, she stepped into the vault and came back quickly with the box. "Could you step over to the cashier's window, Mr. Benson?" she asked with a smile. He did so and she placed the box in front of him. Lazarus opened it and took out two large velvet bags and a few envelopes and put them in his pocket. "About the bill, sir," asked the cashier, "how will you pay—in cash or check?"

"I'll pay for my lodging and whatever is owed by my brother."

The cashier fingered the buttons on the adding machine and said, "That comes to five hundred and eight dollars, including your bill."

Lazarus said, "I'll pay cash. Do I need a reference?"

The girl smiled. Lazarus counted out the money, then limped to his suitcase, hooked the handle with his cane, and motioned Nancy and Gerald to follow him.

"The elevator is this way," said the manager, pointing the way.

Lazarus looked around as if he's never seen the hotel before. "This has to be the world's largest basement," he quipped. They reached the elevator, Lazarus unhooked his cane and with the tip of it he pressed the UP button. The manager reached down and picked up the suitcase. "What floor is it that we go to?" asked Lazarus, forgetfully.

"Fifteen," said the manager, beginning to believe that Lazarus was absent minded.

Lazarus looked at Nancy. "So you are Carol's friend. He spoke highly of you, but I thought you would be older. He did say how beautiful you are."

"Thank you," said Nancy.

117

"What do you do, young fellow?" he asked abruptly, turning to Gerald.

"I am a student. But right now I am trying to get my father out of prison."

"Well, I think we can handle that."

"Are you retired, Mr. Benson?" asked the manager.

"No," said Lazarus as he handed the manager his calling card, "I am on a lecture tour."

Looking up from the card the manager seemed to be impressed. "You are a Doctor of Communications and Criminology!" The elevator door opened and the manager escorted them to the suite of rooms that had been occupied by Carol Benson. "If there is anything we can do to make your stay with us comfortable, just let us know. Oh, and by the way, about this murder you mentioned. If you could keep the name of the hotel out of print . . ."

"I have a feeling you won't hear a word about it," interrupted Lazarus. As the manager was about to leave, Lazarus stopped him. "There is something you can do. Do you know the chief of police?"

"I met him once. They gave a dinner in his honor and made him 'Man of the Year.' "

"Well, you can give him another dinner and take the honor back. Could you call him and tell him that James Benson, the brother of Carol Benson, who he believes to have been murdered, would like the chief to get over here to the hotel pronto. Faster if he can make it!"

"Well, I don't like to get involved."

"Then you don't mind if the hotel does?"

"I'll call him, immediately, from my office."

"You do that," suggested Lazarus, closing the door.

After the manager left the room, Gerald was full of high spirits. "Man," he said, "you're something else. We didn't even recognize you."

Lazarus became stern. "How could you recognize me, since we have never met before?"

The grin left Gerald's face. "I see what you mean."

Lazarus went into the bathroom, then called out to Nancy, "Would you get Mr. Griffen on the phone. Tell him it's urgent and to get over here right away. Tell him to make sure the chief of police comes with him."

Nancy hurried to the phone.

Lazarus opened the closet door and took out the suits hanging there and put them on the bed. He then cleared out the dresser drawers, opened a small suitcase and put a few articles from it into the dresser.

There was a knock at the door. "Get that, young man," shouted Lazarus.

Gerald opened the door. There stood the manager with a waiter in a white coat who pushed a table into the room. On it were soft drinks, a bottle of wine, fruits and flowers, along with an assortment of meats and cheeses. "Compliments of the hotel, sir."

"Thank you," said Lazarus. "Did you make that call to the chief of police?"

"Yes, and he said he'd be right over."

Nancy interrupted, "Gaylord is coming, too!"

"Who's Gaylord?" asked Lazarus.

"Mr. Griffen," answered Nancy.

Lazarus called the waiter over. "Do you know anyone who can use these clothes?" he asked him, pointing to the bed.

"I am not allowed to take anything out of the hotel," said the waiter.

"I'm giving you the stuff. My brother won't be needing it."

"Suppose your brother returns?" asked the manager.

"He's not going to return. I have him in an ice box at the undertaker's parlor."

The manager seemed shocked at the remark.

Nancy spoke up. "I'll give the clothes to The Salvation Army."

"Yeah," said Lazarus, "that's a better idea."

"Well, enjoy your treats," said the manager. "Oh, by the

way, the purse snatcher in front of the hotel was arrested and taken away."

"Thank you for everything," said Lazarus, closing the door after the two men stepped into the hall. Then he limped back into the bedroom.

Nancy asked, "Did you hurt your foot?"

"Yeah," said Lazarus, "I hurt my foot. I bought one shoe too small."

"Why?" asked Gerald.

"So he could limp!" said Nancy, rather disgusted with him.

Minutes later, the phone rang. Lazarus answered the call. "Hello. By all means, send them up." He hung up the receiver. "The pollution is settling in. Our guests have arrived."

"I'm sort of scared. I think I could die," said Nancy.

Lazarus just looked at her. "You leave it to me, but think at all times. Don't be tricked or bullied, either one of you."

Nancy and Gerald sat down on the couch. Lazarus fixed a fast couple plates of food, opened some Cokes and glassed them with ice, then set the treats in front of them. "Just relax," he said. "Now you are going to see two men squirm like they should be wormed." He fixed himself a sandwich and loaded his plate with sweet pickles. "In hotels, when they give you this stuff free, it usually means it's left over from yesterday's buffet." He opened a Coke and drank from the can.

Nancy smiled. "You know it is wonderful to see you play cat and mouse."

"Wrong," said Lazarus. "Just cat."

There was a knock on the door. Lazarus got up, limped to the door, and opened it. Standing there were the two gentlemen. At one glance Lazarus could tell they didn't know what to expect.

"I am Gaylord Griffen, this is Chief Williger."

"Come in."

Griffen seemed surprised to see Nancy and Gerald. "Looks like you're making a habit of coming to hotels with elderly men," said Griffen to Nancy. Then, turning to Gerald, he said, "If I had known you were here I wouldn't have come."

"Why? Does he look that much like his father?" asked Lazarus.

"Sir," said Griffen, "I don't know you. Would you tell me what this is all about? And whatever it is, I think this young man should leave."

Lazarus became annoyed. "I don't know what your problem is with the young man, but I do know that it's my room and I think, on that point, under due process of the law I have a right to say who should or shouldn't be here."

The chief spoke up. "Mr. Benson, I am a busy man. What's this about your missing brother?"

"I didn't say he was missing, I said he was dead! Murdered!"

Both men looked at each other.

"Don't be shocked," smiled Lazarus.

"I am not," said the chief. "I was wondering why you didn't report the news about your brother to the police."

"I didn't think it was necessary to report a crime to someone who already knew about it. Why don't you hear what's to be said before you make your second fatal mistake? You see, the shortest distance between two points is a straight line. That also applies to the truth. It's simple. My brother owed me two hundred thousand dollars. He assured me that if I came here he would have the money." He took his cane and used it to pull up a chair. He sat down, facing the two men. "It's too bad you had to kill the goose that laid the golden way out of your problem."

The chief sat up. "I didn't get your name," he said in a sardonic way.

Lazarus handed him his calling card. Looking at the card the chief said, "Criminologist. Interesting."

"I am James Benson. Carol Benson was my brother."

"Was?" repeated the chief.

"Yes, he is dead, and you know it."

"No," said the chief guardedly. "How would I know?"

"Because you helped kill him!" said Lazarus in a loud voice.

"Now just one minute!" shouted the chief.

"Sit down," said Lazarus, "you are betraying your dignity as an officer. You know, in my research on crime I've discovered that a guilty person is always first to defend himself with indignant remarks. Now, don't get yourself in any deeper. Just listen to facts. If you wish to have an attorney present, there is the phone. But, after hearing the evidence, I don't think you'd want a stranger in on this."

"A stranger?"

"Yes, because before I'm through you won't be able to get an ambulance chaser to take the case. It would ruin his reputation. Now, let's sit down and talk."

"You know you are as rude as your brother!" said Mr. Griffen.

Lazarus could now relax because he knew his disguise was working. He got up and limped over even closer to Griffen, pulling up a chair right next to him. "Well, now that we have established the fact that you did know my brother, I am sure you would like to know why your daughter is here."

"Stepdaughter!" said Nancy

"I am sorry, Gloria."

"Nancy!" said Nancy, annoyed.

"Whatever," replied Lazarus.

"You know, Mr. Griffen, I am sure Nancy can be your saving factor. She and my dead brother worked out a plan that can save face for you and your company and, at the same time, get this young man's father released from prison." Lazarus turned to Nancy. "Did you talk to the district attorney about my brother's plan?"

"I have an appointment with him at five o'clock today," answered Nancy. "And Gaylord knew about your brother's plan," continued Nancy, now most confident in herself.

"Now I must tell you why I am here," said Lazarus.

122

The chief squirmed a little, then said, "I wish you'd tell me why I am here."

"Murder!" said Lazarus.

"What in the hell are you talking about?"

"Well, you won't tell me, so I'll tell you. But in time. First, why am I here? My brother owed me, as I said, two hundred thousand dollars. He asked me to come here so he could pay me the money. He was confident, no doubt, that Mr. Griffen would pay him for his wonderful plan to get a Mr. Gillis out of prison. He paused, reached into his pocket and brought out a notepad, then began searching his pocket for his reading glasses. "My glasses, I can never find them."

"They are on top of your head," chuckled Nancy.

He reached up and put them on. "I don't know why I do that. Folks must think I have a nearsighted skull." He then looked at the paper he had gotten out of his pocket. "Yes, the plan to get a Mr. Gilly . . ."

"Never mind that! What's this about your missing brother?" interrupted the chief.

"My brother seems to be an obsession with you. Maybe you would tell me what happened?"

"Why me?" asked the chief.

"Because you two gentlemen were the last to see him alive, and you, sir," he said, turning to the chief, "were the last to see him dead." He paused. "But there is a way out as long as I get my two hundred thousand dollars and you follow through with Nancy's and my brother's plan to get Gerald's father out of prison. When the money is paid I will call the mortuary and tell them to ship my brother's body to Maine to be buried in our family plot. Now, two hundred thousand dollars is a small price to pay to rid yourself of perjury and embezzlement charges. And a senseless murder. You see, my brother was a very sick man who had about three or four weeks to live. He had been to Mayo and Johns Hopkins and I guess he thought helping Nancy would be his passport into heaven.

123

My brother was a proud man who didn't want pity from anyone, but he hired several men to stay always at a distance, so if and when the time came, they could take care of him and contact me. The last day he was alive, one of his men was in the hotel garage. He saw your police car drive in, followed by another car which was driven by Mr. Griffen. A lady was with him. They all went into the hotel. Later, this witness saw two men dragging a body to the police car. He became curious as to why a civilian would be helping a police officer make an arrest. If the man was Griffen's friend and the officer was assisting him, why was the body put on the floor of the squad car and not into Mr. Griffen's car? Next question that bothered the witness: what happened to the lady?

"Curiosity got the best of the witness, so he followed the police car. Knowing the officer was sworn to uphold the law, the man wondered why the officer didn't summon paramedics and order an ambulance to take this man to a hospital or a morgue? So the witness followed the police car, at a safe distance, to a lonely, deserted road, then the witness saw the officer throw the body into a ditch and drive off. The man notified me. The body was taken to a mortuary. Now, as soon as I get the two hundred thousand dollars, I call the mortician, then the airport. I take a plane to my destination and my brother's body will be shipped home and buried with honors. And you gentlemen are as free as Mr. Gilly, after you talk to the district attorney.

"Your second set of books plays two parts. Those books can get a man out of prison or, you Mr. Griffen, into prison. And, depending upon what you decide to do, they can make my brother's casket disappear or they can have it opened at court. Gentlemen, need I tell you that murder is a serious charge!

"Now, I have no emotional feelings about the embezzlement, nor do I have any about my brother's death. Perhaps he welcomed death. I am sure it was welcome relief from his pain. On the other hand, I do have an emotional interest in two hundred thousand dollars."

The two men sat dumbfounded.

"You know, to bring disgrace to you two gentlemen would afford me no satisfaction only truth. But keep in mind, gentlemen, this was premeditated murder—two men disposing of a lifeless body. Now, the witness! I have been able to convince him not to get involved as a witness, or he could also wind up a victim. I explained to him, the officer has a thousand reasons to kill a witness. So I gave him money to take a long holiday until after my brother is buried in Maine.

"But again, I remind you that the set of books, which are in safe keeping, could prove in court that Mr. Griffen committed perjury and put an innocent man in prison is right here. But following my brother's and Nancy's plan does away with that evidence.

"Now, all I have to do is call the mortuary and instruct the mortician to ship the body out of state. Then, with the two hundred thousand dollars I get on an afternoon plane. That's why this meeting was called early. I am sure you will see the logic.

"Meanwhile, I will check out of the hotel. I'll have my plane ticket. The chief will escort me to the plane. I will board the plane on the field so that I don't have to open my bags through security. I think it might be unwise to open bags with two hundred thousands dollars in them." He turned to Nancy. "You meet with the district attorney at five."

Nancy came out of her spellbound trance and said, "Based on our conversation on the phone, I would say that he will go along with Carol's plan."

Nancy saw that the two men were buying all that was said. She shook her head in disbelief.

"Well, Mr. Griffen," said Lazarus, getting up and pouring a Coke, "I am sure you have two hundred thousand in a safety deposit box?"

Griffen stood up, as if in a daze, then asked, "Was a diamond found on your brother?"

"Not to my knowledge.

"Well, Griffen, there's nothing more to be said. I expect you back here in one hour."

"When does Mr. Griffen get his records back?" asked the chief.

"You'll have your books after I'm safely on my way, and you've had your talk with the D.A. Lazarus became didactic. "Believe me, your deepest imagination is not capable of competing with a mind that knows and understands the roots of crime. Should you change your mind about releasing Mr. Gilly from prison, remember that Nancy can become a state witness and still nail you both. If that should happen, I will return and testify about the death of my brother.

"Well children," Lazarus said to Nancy and Gerald, "maybe you'd like to step into the bedroom and freshen up, so we can have a bite of lunch." Then, turning to Griffen, who still stood, dumbfounded, he said, "One hour, gentlemen. I have reservations for Chicago. Right now, Nancy, Gerald, and I are going to lunch."

It was less than thirty minutes when Griffen and the chief returned. Griffen handed Lazarus a briefcase, then asked, "You want to count it?"

"I don't have to because you are not capable of doing what you think you are capable of."

Nancy smiled. "I think I would look if I were you."

Nancy opened the case and saw packages of bills. "You see, child, there is honor among thieves," he remarked as he peeked into the bag. He got up from the table.

The police car drove him to the gate at the airport. Lazarus got out and handed Nancy an envelope. "A wedding gift," he said.

Nancy kissed Lazarus on the cheek. "I hate to see you go!"

"I'll be back if you need me. Be happy and, above all, know in your heart you'll always be in mine. You are my reason for living. And don't concern yourself with the grim reaper. He comes when the time is right and needs no assistance."

An airport assistant helped Lazarus. Lazarus gave him his ticket and quickly got on the plane. His heart was aching, but his eyes were already looking for new adventures.

CHAPTER EIGHT

Even though time sometimes appears to stand still, it mostly marches inexorably on. But it becomes absolutely frightening when the past returns and a particular time has to be relived. Old acquaintances show up with that most haunting phrase: "Remember when . . . ." I've found that it is best to say to them, "No, I don't" It saves bringing back hurts and regrets.

Rediscovering Charlie Price, the barker, was such an excursion into the past. The years hadn't changed him much. He was still a carnival man at heart, though he was now in a new business. He had become a travel agent, which gave him a more intimate contact with (as he put it) the suckers. He would charter a plane and take a hundred tourists to all parts of the world on a fifteen day jaunt, which meant that if you dropped your camera you missed two countries. But it gave Charlie a chance to see the world and, at the same time, to appease the larceny in his heart by taking his groups into stores and shops where he had previously made deals with the merchants. They paid him a percentage of the take for bringing his little lambs in to buy inferior merchandise and be slaughtered with jacked-up prices.

To Charlie it had the feel of the carnival, with the tourists being the freaks. In fact, it was better than the carnival because the freaks paid him to take them to the side show. It was also like being on a merry-go-round, with all the packing and unpacking, washing your own clothes, living in cheap hotels, and traveling in circles. Best of all, he was able to make use of his barker's gift of gab. But if he were to take an aptitude test to find out what he was best suited for, it would come out "jail." After thirty years he was still deficient in just about everything positive, including common sense. As Lazarus had once said, "If Charlie were to auction off his good qualities, there wouldn't be an opening bid."

When acting as a guide to his groups, Charlie had his own explanations for all the sights and sounds of Paris. He would point out famous landmarks, but his descriptions, though spoken through the filter of rapturous eloquence, were never accurate. He pointed out to his people that the pamphlets covered the facts. But to him the historians were deficient and he managed to imbue all things he described with his own drama and atmosphere. At the Louvre, for instance, Charlie related inside information about Van Gogh cutting off his ear.

Charlie's version went like this. "There was this lady of the evening who was loved by Van. All she wanted from him on her birthday was something small and inexpensive, like an ear. Well, he cut it off and gave it to her. She said to him, 'It's the wrong ear.' So he went to the hospital, had it sewed back on, then borrowed the doctor's knife and cut off his other ear. He tied a scarf around his head and took the new ear to the girl. She called him 'stupid' and said, 'I never want to see you again!' Well, the real tragedy was that Van never heard a word she said."

Charlie's mind was strong but narrow, resplendent with far out glittering sentiments that were mostly imaginary. But his groups seemed to find him likeable and dismissed most of what he said as a joke, believing he was only trying to entertain them.

The one nice place on the tour was a good hotel in Paris, which always meant a big party, a chance to rest, time to send things out to be cleaned and pressed, and an opportunity to do some real sightseeing. On one particular tour the lobby of that elegant hotel in Paris was cluttered with luggage, if it could be called that. Mostly it was paper shopping bags and steamer trunks and footlockers made of cardboard and tin—

a sight far from the elegance of travel, even twenty years ago. Today's air traveler's standards are below those of the bus traveler in the 1940's, when the men and women all looked spiffy. Now, the women's wardrobes look like blue light specials from the Goodwill Store, and the men all must have blind tailors. Their clothes are a cross between Brooks and Ringling Brothers.

The guests in Charlie's group were all loud and obnoxious. They all wanted attention at the same time, some complaining about lost baggage. He had to explain that their luggage couldn't be lost since they traveled on a chartered plane. He was busy, at the same time, assigning rooms and handing out keys. Each member of the group received an envelope, a guide book, and a list of the special shopping places. As soon as Charlie assigned a person to a room he marked it down on the list on his clipboard and yelled out the name of the next wandering zombie. Everyone in the group was at least one step beyond a displaced person. They all looked like impoverished aristocrats, with as much taste as a night club salad. Throughout the whole process they argued and complained about credit cards, the cell-like rooms and the rudeness of the bell boys who complained, in turn, about the cheap tips they received for pushing carts fourteen feet to the elevator and then fifty feet to the room where they would have to lift two small handbags.

Adding to the confusion this particular time were two other groups who were checking in at the same time because one group's plane had been late and the other's buses had been held up in traffic. Travel at a cheap rate is one mass of stringy hair and smelly bodies, with everyone making insulting remarks and forgetting they are guests in a foreign country.

There are those who try their handbook French on bell boys who speak better English than the clods who keep reminding them that they are Americans. But the Americans are not alone. The Japanese are the worst offenders; they feel everything they encounter is an invasion.

131

Charlie tried to be orderly, but everyone was unhappy, especially about their rooms. In his group were Mr. and Mrs. Gaylord Griffen. He is the big real estate developer who lives with the knowledge that he killed a man five years earlier. He had aged considerably since that time. His wife, Mildred, was arguing with Price. "You told us you would get us a room with a view when we got to Paris."

"The booking got mixed up. They had us booked for tomorrow. They are doing their best to accommodate everyone. Here are your keys. The room will be lovely. After all, you are in the best hotel in Paris."

She snatched the keys from Charlie, then demanded that the bell boy fetch their baggage.

The bell boy, the most courteous they had met so far on the tour, yelled, "You have to wait your turn, lady. I am not a robot slave!" Then he jabbered insulting remarks in French.

Mrs. Griffen became indignant. "I am a woman of few words, and you will get all of them! I hope they have decent bathrooms."

"The bathroom is out of this world, which makes it nice but a little inconvenient," Charlie assured Mrs. Griffen, trying to lighten things up a bit. He shook his head.

I often wonder why people travel. There is never one face with a friendly expression or any other sign that they are enjoying their excursion. The service and hotel employees do their work grudgingly. The concierge dominates the scene and only acts civil for a price.

One guest, a lady elegantly dressed for the evening, made her way through the turmoil and referred to the Americans as "the pizza set." She was particularly amused that they ordered California wine when they were in Paris because they refused to drink the domestic stuff.

As the elevator door opened, Lazarus came face to face with Mr. Griffen, who was startled and stepped back to let Lazarus and the other hotel guests off the lift. Lazarus stepped aside and said, "Pardon me."

Griffen was in shock. Mildred took his arm. "Are you all right?" she asked.

Griffen walked to a high back chair and all but fell into it. A couple in their party tried to assist him.

"Is he all right?" asked Charlie. "He's as pale as a ghost."

Griffen was wild-eyed as he glanced around. It was as if something had taken possession of his soul; he seemed horror stricken. The blank smile on his face was empty. His eyes were lifeless. He looked as if he had seen something hideous.

Mildred turned to Mr. Price. "Is our room ready yet? I think he should lie down and rest."

"Yes," said Charlie. "I'd better get a doctor."

"No," insisted Mildred, "he'll be all right. He's had these spells before. He gets them when he is exhausted."

Charlie eagerly inquired, "I wonder what brought it on? He saw this guy getting off the elevator and suddenly he went into shock."

Mildred was holding her husband's hand and trying to be cheerful in order to aliviate his condition somewhat. "You'll be all right," she assured him. She turned to Charlie. "Let's get him to the room."

They helped Griffen to his feet. He was pale and clumsy and he continually glanced about as if he were expecting some evil force, some vivid terror to attack him. Everything was vague to him. Once in their room, Mildred assured Mr. Price that all was under control and that her husband was doing fine.

After Charlie left the room she locked the door and turned to Gaylord. "What happened?" she asked with great interest.

"Did you lock the door?" he asked, still perplexed.

His wife became irritated. "For God's sake, will you tell me what happened?"

"He is alive!"

"Who is alive?"

"That man I thought I killed," he said in a loud whisper.

Mildred became exasperated. "Oh, for heaven's sake, you are not going to start on that again! You are going to keep on that subject until you are back in the hospital again. You have been fine for two years." She became disheartened. "I don't think I can go through that again."

"This time I saw him. He had a beard but it was the same man," said Griffen.

"Gaylord, the dead do not return. It is all your imagination. Besides, I've told you, over and over, I don't believe you harmed that man in any way. As his brother said, he was dying anyway. Besides, if you did, it was an accident." A gloom suddenly pervaded the room. There came a knock on the door. Mildred turned to Griffen as she walked to the door. "Now pull yourself together!

"Who is there?"

"It's me, Charlie Price."

She opened the door. Charlie entered the room, carrying a tray with hot coffee, two sandwiches and a bottle of wine. "I brought some food and coffee. The dining rooms don't open until seven, but I managed something. If you eat some of this it will help. Better yet, I'll open the bottle of wine." He grabbed the bottle and uncorked it. "The bus ride in from the airport without air conditioning didn't help. That bus company will get a piece of my mind," he said as he opened the bottle. "I saw how the French hate Americans, but it does no good to complain. I'll tell you one thing, it's the last time I ever include France on any of my tours." He walked to the bed where Gaylord was stretched out and handed him a glass of wine. "You feel better?"

"I am O.K.," said Gaylord, with little confidence.

"You know," said Charlie, "I knew there was something wrong when I saw the way you stared at that guy getting off the elevator. It was as if you had seen a ghost. It's that jet lag. You know, I thought I recognized that guy, too. He reminded me of someone from years ago. I even inquired as to who the fellow is. His name is Wallingford. He's a diplomat, here on a peace mission. I figured I must have seen his picture in the newspaper, but never paid attention to who he was. It's like seeing a movie star. You are not sure who it is, but they remind you of someone you know."

Gaylord snapped out of his stupor. "Yeah, that could be what it was," said Griffen, not quite convinced, but ready to accept anything to relieve the shock and regain his senses.

"Now you rest," said Charlie as he walked to the door. "You both take a little rest. If you feel like it, you can join the group later and we'll see Paris. This place has sights beyond comparison to any place you've ever been, even though the people are miserable. Get some hot coffee and some food into you. Better still, have a few glasses of wine. That will help you relax."

Charlie's cordiality and concern helped convince them that all was well. Mildred thanked him for his thoughtfulness. After he left she locked the door.

Gaylord stretched on the bed and looked extremely apologetic. "I am sorry, but the way that fellow looked, even with a beard, I was sure it was the same man, Mildred."

She started unpacking her things. "You and I are the only ones who know about him, except Nancy, Gerald, and his brother. They have all kept their word and nothing has ever been said. But you know I instinctively feel that the chief had a part in stealing my ring. We searched that room high and low and never found one glimpse of it."

Griffen was out of his fearful stupor and apathy had settled in. In a minute he succumbed to sleep. Mildred finished unpacking, lay down beside him and quickly fell asleep.

When they awoke, neither mentioned the incident. There was even a closer intimacy between them; they both lost the dull radiation of gloom that had previously surrounded them. During dinner, Mildred took her handkerchief and dabbed her eyes which trickled with a tear. But she quickly returned to a cheerful mood. She seemed to have stored everything in a dark, painful recess of her mind. They were in Paris, the city of lights, with music and excitement, and at least a momentary bit of happiness for a consciousness haunted by morbid memories.

First, Charlie Price, then Mr. and Mrs. Griffen, the hotel was quickly becoming a convention center for former Lazarus' victims. Whatever caper he had in the works would soon have to be canceled. But that wasn't the end of the list.

It was mid afternoon when Lazarus got off the elevator and was walking through the lobby to the concierge's desk. Suddenly, the lobby door opened. In came a flamboyant, ostentatious lady, escorted by a few friends. She was jovially striding past Lazarus when she suddenly stopped, as if she had run into an invisible wall. She hesitated a second, then turned and took a good, long gander at him. Lazarus ignored her. It was Sarah.

Her friends were concerned. "What's the matter, something wrong?" asked her lady friend.

"That handsome gentleman, for a second I thought I recognized him." Then, seeing the assistant manager speaking with the bell captain, she walked over to him. "I don't mean to be rude, but do you happen to know who that gentleman is over there, talking to the concierge? Isn't he a movie star?"

The assistant manager gave a quick glance in Lazarus' direction and replied, "That, madam, is Mr. Wallingford. I believe he is with the American Diplomatic Corps. Shall I introduce you to him?"

"No, no, that won't be necessary. Has he been here long?"

"About six months," replied the assistant manager. "I'll be glad to introduce you."

"No," said Sarah, "I was just curious. I thought it was Maurice Chevalier."

The assistant manager thought for a moment. "He is dead!"

"So is the guy I was thinking of." She turned and entered the elevator.

After the doors closed Lazarus walked over to the assistant manager. "Did that lady inquire about me?"

"Yes, she thought you were a movie star."

Lazarus smiled. "How flattering."

The next day Lazarus called a theatrical agency and hired a beautiful actress and two children. That evening, in the dining room, Sarah didn't take her eyes off Lazarus. She was searching for one habit that would match something that would convince her that it was really Larry. But, as I have said before, one of his rules was to change every identifying characteristic that was a carry-over from a previous disguise.

Lazarus was most attentive to his attractive lady companion. Suddenly, the door from the kitchen opened and in came a boy and girl, age five and six, carrying a large cake with candles and the words "Happy Anniversary" on it. The waiter took the cake from them and placed it on the table. The little girl first hugged the lady and said, "Happy anniversary, Mother," then she gave a big hug to Lazarus, saying, "Happy anniversary, Papa."

Seeing the happy little farce was a family get-together, Sarah shrugged her shoulders and said to her three companions, "Well, we all make mistakes."

Sarah didn't know that her waiter and captain were also actors. With a thick French accent, the waiter said, "A beautiful family!"

"You know him?"

"Mr. Wallingford? Oui! For about seven years."

"Do they live at the hotel?"

"Only, Mr. Wallingford. The family lives in the suburbs. His work keeps him at the hotel. It's all top secret."

Sarah seemed to lose interest in Lazarus. It couldn't be Larry.

But two days later Lazarus noticed someone following him, so he hired a cab to drive him to the U.S. Embassy. He got out of the cab and stepped inside the door. A few minutes later, in came the man who was following him. Lazarus grabbed the man's arm, gave it a twist, and pulled him into a small alcove. "Now," said Lazarus, "Why are you following me?"

"I am a private detective. But not a very good one!"

"And I am with the diplomatic corps. I have immunity. Nothing you find out is of value. Now, who hired you?"

"I can't reveal the identity of my client."

"You will," said Lazarus, adding pressure to the arm, "or I'll take you upstairs and in five minutes your license will be revoked. Now, who are you working for?"

The man was in pain. Finally, he said, "She is Sarah Halsted."

Lazarus released his grip and chuckled. "The very woman we have under surveillance."

"What do you mean?" asked the man, rather amazed, and rubbing his arm.

"She is a Russian spy!"

"She is an American."

"Working for the Russians."

"No!" said the little man, adjusting his coat.

"She sells information and when she is arrested, you will be an accomplice."

"I am a private detective."

"*Was*," said Lazarus, making the word a very positive threat. "Don't you take time to investigate who you are working for?"

"I am just doing my job," said the detective, very nervously.

"Well, you keep doing it and you'll be doing time." Then Lazarus changed his manner and became friendly. "I didn't hurt you, did I?"

"Well, you didn't help me any."

"Sit down."

They sat on a marble bench. "Now, what did she want to know?" asked Lazarus as he reached into his pocket and brought out a pack of cigarettes, offering one to the little man. "You want a smoke?"

"Ah, American cigarettes! Haven't had one since the war. Merci beaucoup."

"Take a pack, I can get more at the PX."

"Merci," he said, offering one to Lazarus.

"No thanks, I don't smoke." The little man seemed surprised. "Now what did this spy want to know!"

"She hired me to find out all about you."

Lazarus smiled. "And you took the job? Don't you know what can happen to you for investigating a diplomat? They will open the Bastille and give you a private room."

"No!"

"Now what did she want to know?"

The detective took out a little note pad. "How long have you been in Paris?"

"Ten years."

"How long have you been married?"

"Seven years. Two children. I haven't been on leave in the States for eight years."

The little fellow was busy writing. "Why are you living in the hotel?"

"Because my house burned down three years ago. My wife and children live with her mother."

"She also wants to know, do you like jewelry?"

"I own a gold wedding band. My wife has a one carat diamond engagement ring and a diamond wedding band. What else?"

"Do you read horoscopes?"

"I am too busy with today to think about tomorrow. What else?"

"That's about all. I'll report this to her."

"No, wait. The Russians pay her a lot of money. You wait a few days and then really give her a bill. She can afford it. Charge her enough so you can take a trip to the south of France for the summer. It won't cost you a dime. Tell her it costs a lot to get this information from secret sources. Then get off the case or you know what's going to happen to you!" He dismissed the man.

From then on Sarah still stared at Lazarus and wondered.

Meanwhile, Lazarus was still being stalked by his other victims. Charlie Price was seated with a woman at the bar off the lobby. It was after eleven in the evening, the only time Charlie was able to get away from the demands of those in

139

his group. As he sat at the bar he noticed three men at a table, one of whom he was very interested in. The lady with Charlie didn't mind his lack of attention to her at first, but she finally became annoyed.

"Why do you keep staring at that table?"

Charlie apologized. "I'm sorry," he said, "but that one guy at that table looks just like a guy who used to work with me when I was in show business. He was called The Great Lazarus. He did a hell of an act. He would die on stage. The doctors would pronounce him dead, then he would come back to life."

"Sounds like an evening with you!" She took a sip of her drink and said, "Why don't you go over and ask him his name? He look's like he's an American."

"Naw, that was a long time ago. Besides, I've inquired. He's a diplomat of some sort, here on some kind of peace mission."

"Well then, stop staring at him!" suggested the lady.

"I know it's rude, but if it's him, sooner or later he is going to recognize me. Boy, it sure looks like him."

The three men got up from the table and walked past Charlie, who spoke as Lazarus walked by. "Good night," said Charlie.

Lazarus glanced at Charlie. "Good night," he responded. Then he gave a smile and bowed to the lady. "Madam," he said and kept right on walking.

The lady with Charlie said, "Well, why didn't you ask him his name?"

"No, that guy has too much class, nothing show business about him."

It was at breakfast the next day that Charlie was seated with Mr. and Mrs. Griffen. Gaylord nudged his wife. "That fellow over there, that's him."

Mildred put on her glasses. "Where?"

"Don't stare, but he is at the table over in the corner."

After a good look, she said, "There are three men at that table, which one in particular?"

"The one with the beard. He is looking over in this direction."

"Well, I never saw him before. My God, Gaylord, are you going to start that again?"

"If he didn't have the beard, who does he remind you of?"

"He reminds me of a man without a beard."

Charlie took up the conversation. "That guy must remind everyone of someone. I thought I knew him, too."

"I wonder who he really is?" asked Mr. Griffen.

"It's J. P. Wallingford. He's with the U.S. Diplomatic Service, here on a peace mission. I told you that before."

Just about this time Lazarus recognized, not only Charlie, but also Mr. and Mrs. Griffen, but he didn't acknowledge them. He paid his check by signing the tab. He must have given a generous tip, the waiter couldn't seem to do enough for him. He left quickly as if he were late to an important appointment.

That night was chilly and misty. Earlier, the skyline had danced with flickering lights, but now it had lost its magic. In the distance, Rue Montmartre was a vague haze. The trees wore a soggy coat, the streets were a shiny black, the shrubs had lost their green color and stood like dark alien objects. The hotel was wrapped in silence, the guests in deep sleep, exhausted from sightseeing and shopping. Charlie was seated at the desk, going over bills and the itinerary for the day about to be born and given the name "Hectic." The hour was two. He was out of wine and the girl he had been with had left for another appointment.

There was a light tapping. He walked to the door, trying to see who it was through the peep hole. He inquired, "Who's there?"

"Mr. Price," whispered the voice, "open up!"

He opened the door as far as the safety latch would reach. Standing there was the bearded man.

"It's me, Lazarus, open up!"

Charlie unlatched the door and opened it. "Well, I'll be! I knew it was you. You are a hell of an actor!"

"I just stopped by for a minute."

141

Charlie put on his bathrobe. "You know," he said, "I knew if it was you, you wouldn't snub me."

"I had no intentions of doing that, but the work I am in, the minute I speak to a stranger, the CIA starts asking questions. This town is lousy with spies."

"It's lousy without them," said Charlie.

"How have you been doing?"

"Oh, fair to middle, as they say. I'm in the travel business."

"I saw your little group."

"Some are problems, a few have big money. A little nerve shattering at times, but it's a living. I gave up show business but not travel. Well, it's good to see you after all these years," said Charlie, giving Lazarus a friendly pat, "even though it took me some time to forgive you for what you did to me."

"I suppose you never gave a thought to what you did to me?" replied Lazarus.

"Yeah, I guess we had a good thing going. I should have paid you more."

"It wasn't the money. It's just that one day I tasted food and realized you needed money to buy it. What did you do after I left the show?"

"I did all right. I hired Iron Jaw McGirk. A great attraction. Not like you but they came to see him."

"I never heard of him. What kind of act did he do?"

"Well, his wife would stand in front of him and fire a gun and he would catch the bullet in his teeth."

"You're kidding?" said Lazarus in disbelief.

"Well, his wife was a slight of hand expert. She would pass live ammunition around the audience, then load the gun. But she was so quick they didn't see her switch the bullets to blanks—and she did it wearing gloves. Well, anyway, she finds out McGirk is playing around with the Indian Rubber Girl. She was a contortionist and his wife thought that this was stretching things a bit too far. One afternoon she put a real bullet in the gun and blew his head off. Since she didn't have an encore they arrested her. You know, it was the funniest

142

trial ever. The prosecuting attorney tried to mix her up on the witness stand, but she was a calm baby. He asked her if she knew Iron Jaw was playing around. She said, 'He always did, but that's no reason to blow a hole in my meal ticket. Times are tough. You put up with what you have to.' The judge asked her how long she had been doing the act. She said, 'Ten years.' The judged then asked, 'And this is the first time he missed?' 'Obviously,' she told him. Well, the court went in to gales of laughter and the judge wound up dismissing the case. She was a beauty. The most perfect body you ever laid eyes on. But, you know, there is a law of retribution. She was in her motel cleaning her gun and it went off and killed her. Now, if she could have pulled your act I would have hired her. By the way, you still do the old act?"

Lazarus shook his head, regretfully. "No place for that kind of act these days. People see too much death as it is in the movies and on TV."

"Well," said Charlie, "it's good to be able to see you. You are with the government?"

"Sort of," said Lazarus.

"You don't ever do the old act?"

"Not since vaudeville. It got to be a strain on the old ticker. I was getting too close to death's real door."

"Boy, what a deal for my group to get to see that act! I am giving the farewell party tomorrow night. Boy, what a thing to take home! And it sure would make me a big man with them."

"No way! The risk, as they say, is risky." Lazarus got up.

"O.K. But if you're not doing anything and would like to stop in for a drink, you are welcome. You know, the people are not all goons. We got one fellow who's a diamond merchant. He's kind of big with the society folks here in Paris. In fact, he is giving a party for some of his wealthy friends who live in Paris."

"If he is so rich," asked Lazarus, "why doesn't he have his own plane? Why is he traveling around like a tourist?"

"I guess with all the hardware he carries it makes him less conspicuous.""The jewels immediately caught Lazarus' attention. "If I am not too busy I will stop in."

"It would be like old times," said Charlie.

"I hope not," said Lazarus as he started to the door. "I have an early call, just wanted to say hello." He hesitated for a second. "Oh, by the way, don't spread it around that I was up here. And remember that my name is Wallingford and we are not old friends. I was more than likely followed, as it is. Besides, I have a lady waiting."

"Oh, I see what you mean," said Charlie with a chuckle and a wink. "Still the old Don Juan with the ladies?"

"No, more like Don Two, at my age."

Charlie opened the door and bid Lazarus good night. "Oh, by the way," said Charlie, "you sure put on a great disguise."

Lazarus returned to his room, but he didn't go to sleep right away. He was giving thought to the party, a chance to make acquaintance with some of the diamond folks. But there was one big risk factor—the Griffens were going to be there. He had taken many chances before, but he couldn't pull the death act on the Griffens again. There was also the possibility that Sarah might show up. But, still, the thought of the jewels intrigued him. He finally fell asleep.

The party was an elegant affair. The people that Charlie spoke of must have had a lot of money. It was certain that Charlie didn't have such good taste, and couldn't have afforded it if he did. The small ballroom on the top floor of the hotel had been rented for the affair. A string quartet played waltzes and minuets, all in the French style. The champagne flowed, but it was too quiet for some of the Americans, one or two of whom were trying to put some life into the gig. Charlie was dressed in his best tux. The diamond folks were in the latest Paris' fashions.

Suddenly, Lazarus appeared in full dress. He was really handsome and distinguished looking. In fact, some of the ladies were almost in a swoon. He was most proper when introduced, as was Charlie, who brought out his best vocabulary and diction. Each word was poetry. When Lazarus was offered champagne he asked for ice tea. When he joined a conversation about world affairs he cast everyone in an hypnotic spell. Abruptly, however, a change came over him when he saw the Griffens standing at the door. But he quickly regained his composure and continued his conversation.

Charlie interrupted, taking Lazarus by the arm and walking him over to the Griffens. "Mr. Wallingford, I want you to meet Mr. and Mrs. Griffen. Mr. Griffen is in the construction business. He is the fellow you gave such a scare," said Charlie as he walked away.

Lazarus bowed, kissed Mildred's hand, then shook Gaylord's. "What part of the States are you from?" asked Lazarus.

"A little town outside of K.C.," Griffen answered.

After a very few moments of idle chat, Lazarus searched out Charlie, for he was sure Griffen recognized him. "Charlie, you have a nice party, I have to be going. I have a dinner engagement."

"Gee, you just got here. I thought it would be entertaining if you just told the folks about our good old days."

Lazarus could see that Charlie had been hitting the grape a little hard and his drunk's tongue was getting loose. "Come with me," said Lazarus. He led him out on to the balcony. "Look," said Lazarus, "I have to leave and you forget the so-called 'good old days.'"

Charlie became angry. "Well, come on," he said, in a rather loud voice, "you are not that good. You know, I never did forget how you walked out on the show. It wasn't very professional. Another thing, you were acting great until Mr. and Mrs. Griffen came in. What's the big deal? How come he thinks he knows you?" Charlie started to move back in to the party room. "Why don't we just go in and find out?"

Lazarus grabbed Charlie. "Look, Charlie, you are drunk."

"I am not. I was having a good time until you pulled this stunt. You know, I never did like you." With that remark he drew back and tried to take a swing at Lazarus. Instead of hitting Lazarus he lost his balance and his momentum flung him forward. Before Lazarus could grab him he went over the low railing and plunged ten floors to the pavement.

Lazarus stood in disbelief. When he looked up, Griffen was standing in the doorway. Lazarus shouted, "For God sakes, man, don't just stand there, call security. There has been an accident!"

Griffen stared at Lazarus and said, "There was no accident, I saw you push that man off the balcony."

Mrs. Griffen grabbed her husband. "What are you saying? You saw nothing!"

"I know that man. He robbed me of two hundred thousand dollars," Griffen yelled. Then he turned and grabbed Lazarus. "You didn't think I recognized you, did you?"

Mrs. Griffen was beside herself.

Lazarus pushed Griffen away and said to him in a low voice, "What about your attempt to murder me? You are trying to slander me. I did not push that man!"

Mrs. Griffen turned to the guests who had gathered. "Don't pay any attention to my husband, he is a very sick man. He doesn't know what he is saying."

"Oh yes I do! And I will see that this man goes to jail to pay for the crime he has just committed."

Mildred looked at Gaylord in disbelief. She was calm as she spoke. "Gaylord, I have tried to understand you, but," she was now in tears, "think of what you are doing. You believe this man to be Mr. Benson. If he is, then you are in the clear. He is alive and you should be grateful you can now lead a normal life. Mr. Gilly is free. Your daughter has given you a lovely grandson. If it wasn't for Mr. Benson, maybe she wouldn't even be alive. If this is that man, there are no more ghosts. Now, tell these people that you didn't see this man throw Mr. Price over that balcony."

Before Griffen could speak, there came a voice from the back of the room. Lazarus looked toward the door. He was stunned.

It was Sarah. She strode in like a demon, pointing her finger at Lazarus.

"That man is a murderer!" she shouted.

"Who is this woman?" asked Lazarus, defying her accusation.

Sarah rudely pushed the guests aside and walked up to Lazarus. Face to face they glared at each other. "I am Sarah Halsted," she said egotistically. "My apartment is across the court. I heard loud voices coming from this balcony. I looked through my opera glasses and saw this man throwing another man's body off the balcony."

Lazarus knew she was vicious, but had not expected this. He shook his head as he saw the blazing hate burning in her piglike eyes. "Madam, you are liar," he shouted.

The two security guards and a gendarme who had been stationed on the floor by the hotel management, knowing there would be guests with valuable jewels, stepped forward. The gendarme spoke English and suggested that Lazarus explain what happened at headquarters. He put handcuffs on Lazarus and took him away.

Lazarus was put on trial. There was no way to defend himself. If he exposed the fact that he could die and return, it would only incriminate him more. His only hope was to be found not guilty. Or, if he were sent to prison, he hoped that Sarah would realize she was sending an innocent man to death and recant her testimony before the death sentence was carried out. If none of this happened he hoped to be able to use the old act—die, be taken from his cell, then find a means to escape.

All in all, the trial was a mockery. Justice was swift. Sarah showed no compassion. She did not even care if he was Larry King, the hate in her heart was so deadly she would have given testimony against anyone who had any resemblance to the man who suckered her out of three million dollars. There was no one to vouch for his character. His only escape was as The Great Lazarus.

The jury brought in the verdict: guilty. Then, in accordance with the matters submitted to his judgement, the judge placed a black napkin on top of his white wig and pronounced the death sentence. Lazarus was taken to a Paris prison to be hanged.

CHAPTER NINE

When I received the letter from Lazarus, giving me all the details of the trial, I couldn't believe it. So I threw a couple of things that might be useful into a couple of bags and booked passage on the first available flight to Paris. Of course, I knew that Sarah had lied on the witness stand.

When I arrived at the hotel I received a most pleasant surprise. I heard the name of Nancy Griffen being paged in the lobby. I sought her out and introduced myself. I really felt that I already knew her from all that Lazarus had told me. She was even more lovely than I had expected.

"I am Jim Lawson, a friend of The Great Lazarus, whom you know as Mr. Carol Benson."

Nancy smiled and extended her hand. "I am glad you are here. When my mother called me and said she was sure they had arrested Mr. Benson for murder, I flew right over to see if I could do something to help. I simply don't believe that he killed anyone."

"Nor do I," I agreed as I led her away from the hotel desk.

"Do you think we could go out to the prison and talk with him?" asked Nancy, rather anxiously.

"I don't think so. Even with my press credentials I doubt if I could get in. I think they have a strict rule that only blood relatives can visit prisoners on death row."

"Oh, God, that phrase sounds so final!"

"Not to me."

"Not really to me, either," said Nancy as if she were sorry

she sounded so hopeless. "We both know he is a dickens, but his good overshadows his little bit of bad."

"Why didn't Mr. Griffen step in and help," I asked out of curiosity.

"He couldn't. The minute he thought he recognized Mr. Benson, Mother said he went haywire. Instead of being grateful for all Benson did, he turned against him. I guess the guilt of thinking you killed a man is not easy to live with."

"But if they go through with this," I said, "he will be living with the guilt of another man's death."

"I know," said Nancy. "But I guess the more you do to help someone see the light, the quicker they are to blow your's out."

I looked at Nancy and smiled. "I think old Lazarus has gotten to you. You sound just like him."

"He did teach me to think and reason."

I asked her to come to my room. "I think we can both help. I have some incriminating evidence against Sarah Halsted. It is something you should hear."

She accepted my invitation. Once in the room I opened my suitcase, took out a tape recorder and played a tape for Nancy. It was the confession that Sarah had made to her young lover when she planned to kill Lazarus. More, important, she admitted that she had murdered two other husbands.

We both felt that if I gave the recording to Sarah she would, in turn, admit that she had lied on the witness stand. If she refused I would turn her confession over to the proper authorities back in the States. It was a Mexican stand-off—her life or his.

Nancy was surprised to learn that Lazarus had been married to Sarah under the name of Larry King, but understood why Sarah had lied on the stand. It was hate and revenge, much the same as the emotions that propelled Griffen. But the intrigue had now reached its limit. Neither of us could figure out why Lazarus had not defended himself. All he would have had to do was say that he had once been married to

Sarah. But then, being the gentleman he was, strange as he was, he probably thought Sarah would step forth at the last minute and admit that she had lied. Since she didn't do this we figured he must be relying on his death act to escape hanging, then hoping to find another way to escape prison.

At first, I thought Nancy would be unable to conceal her emotions. She wanted to demand a new trail, introducing this new evidence. And what better character witness than a girl he had saved from committing suicide who could also testify that Lazarus had helped free Mr. Gilly from prison. But immediately, I saw in Nancy a lady with great simplicity of manner and courtesy, and marvelous powers of patience, endurance, and affection.

After a few seconds of thought she said, "I have a wonderful idea! My mother and Mr. Griffen have made friends with Mrs. Halsted. I find her terribly unpleasant, myself. I think she should carry a turkey with her in case she ever needs spare parts, but I'll try to win her over and give a party in her honor. I'll invite, without her knowledge, every official who has anything to do with French law. I'll turn the dining room into a court room. They will all hear her confession. That will be quicker and more effective than a new trial!"

So Nancy started moving a mountain and left no stone unturned.

CHAPTER TEN

The prison was a remnant of the hate left over from the French Revolution. In it Lazarus learned lessons of life not taught anywhere else. But the one who should have been there was Sarah. Her wickedness was a deadly poison. Her mind was an emporium of crime and her heart was devoted to evil. She was a statement against humanity. What gratification could she possibly receive from being so cruel?

Lazarus had to struggle to maintain his own principles and thoughts about human nature in between the times he was thinking evil thoughts about her. She was the evil croupier of his confinement.

Never had he been so dejected. The walls of his cell were black with age, and reeked with the pungent smell of three hundred years of sweat and urine. (And, to think, France is the leading exporter of perfume! Perhaps they export too much.) The damp walls were covered with a slimy green moss. The thick doors had a slot to slide a dish thorugh, and he was given one modern utensil, a paper cup, to wash down the slop served in the paper dish. This was his French cuisine. The room where he bathed was filled with tarnished foul vapors of putrid air. His wooden bunk had a straw blanket that smelled from disinfectant. There was no light—just a ray of sun coming in the late afternoon, through a one by two foot opening.

But Lazarus withstood all of this, knowing that if the hour came and Sarah had not recanted her testimony, he would do his death act, and once taken to the morgue he felt confident he could escape. Yet the place depressed Lazarus terribly. Not just the fetid physical environment, but all the corroded minds of the "innocent" criminals who surrounded him. It seemed to be a mystery to all of them why they were there. Murder, rape, and the other crimes they were convicted of were, according to them, caused by the wealthy. And they all seemed to feel that evil offered more glory than good.

The evening of Lazarus' execution finally arrived and Sarah had not changed her testimony. Two hours before he was to be executed, Lazarus sent for a priest. A old monk was sent to his cell and he represented the first bit of kindness that Lazarus had experienced since coming to the prison. But Lazarus could see that the monk was frightened of him. After all, he was a man convicted of murder, what was to keep him from going berserk and bouncing the monk against the wall?

"Do you wish to confess your sins?" the monk asked.

"No, I thought we'd take a walk down the Champs-Elysees," said Lazarus with a chuckle.

The monk put the ribbon around his neck and read from St. John. Suddenly, Lazarus fell back on the cot and made a gurgling sound. The monk recognized the death rattle and ran to the door, yelling for help. The guard quickly opened the heavy door. "Get a doctor!" demanded the monk.

The guard quickly summoned the prison doctor. In seconds the prison physician arrived, accompanied by the warden, who was getting ready for the hanging.

The physician put his stethoscope to his ear and listened to Lazarus' heart. He took out his watch and felt Lazarus' pulse. Then he held the watch up to his ear and shook it. Then he listened again with the stethoscope. After a few moments he slowly removed the instrument from his ears and said to the warden, "I hope what I'm about to say will not cause the state an embarrassment because it has just been beaten out of justice. This man is dead."

The monk put a purple ribbon around his neck and began administering the last rights.

Meanwhile, as this drama was taking place in the prison, Nancy's party was in progress at the hotel. It turned out that this particular date was the only one when all concerned could be present. Dinner was set for six o'clock, something unheard of in French society, but all invited had accepted anyway.

Sarah arrived early because her particular invitation was for 5:30. Nancy greeted her, took her by the arm, told her how charming she looked, and admired her lovely jewels. Then she asked the servants to leave the room and introduced Sarah to me.

"This is Mr. Lawson from America. He is a newsman who works for one of the large syndicates."

As soon as Sarah was seated, Nancy placed a recorder in front of her. "I don't give interviews," retorted the flippant Sarah.

"Oh, it's not an interview, it's a confession you made a few years ago. It is something that can get you a death sentence in two states, Texas and Missouri. It's your choice," I said.

"I beg your pardon," said the indigant Sarah.

"That's what it is," said Nancy, "*your pardon.*"

You could hear the clashing of steel as the two women looked daggers at each other. But Nancy had supernatural strength and didn't back down. She sat down beside Sarah and said, "Now, in a few minutes all the heads of crime and court in Paris will be here. I am sure that once they hear this tape the United States Embassy will hold you and notify the authorities in the States. That is, unless Mr. Wallingford is set free. You must get the court to do this by telling them that the death of Charlie Price was accidental. All you have to do is admit your perjury. Tell them you couldn't have seen what was going on out on the balcony because you were standing at the back of the ballroom. Now, there will be no wrangling, no idle words, just an old-fashioned confession."

"May I ask where you got this so-called 'confessions!' "

I said, "It was given to me by Mr. King, whom you now know as Mr. Wallingford."

Sarah stood up. "Damn him! I knew it was him. What does he have to do with you two?"

"Please sit down, Mrs. Halsted," commanded Nancy. "You see, Mr. Wallingford is my dear friend—our dear friend. I know him as Mr. Benson and I intend to keep our friendship alive no matter what his name is. So that you don't have to inconvenience your memory," she said as she reached over and pressed the "play" button on the recorder.

"Shut it off!" shouted Sarah. "I know what's on that tape. I recited it over and over in my sleep."

"Well, so you can get a good night's sleep, all you have to do is confess that you were once married to Mr. Wallingford and you lied to get even with him. It's the only way you can save yourself," Nancy explained.

"Your Mr. Wallingford's right name is Larry Williams," said Sarah, smugly.

"No, his name is Carol Benson," replied Nancy.

"No," I said, "you are both wrong. His name is Lazarus."

"I don't think he knows who he is," suggested Sarah. "What about the recording?"

"We have no need for it if you do what we ask. It becomes yours to destroy or to repent by. It's the only copy. Nancy then showed some compassion. "I don't know what he did or didn't do to you, but he doesn't deserve to die for something he *didn't* do. Whatever your grievance is, two weeks in that prison is punishment enough."

I said to her, "There is an even better reason—no court has any desire to see an innocent man die."

Nancy became gentle but firm. "Now, when everyone gets here, and I hope it's soon because time is running out, you remorsefully insist that what you did was prompted by jealousy. Now you realize that your pride was no more than animal passion. I am sure every Frenchman will understand. If you don't confess, they will hear you admit that you planned once before to kill him just as you had killed your previous two husbands."

156

The door opened and Mr. and Mrs. Griffen walked in. Nancy stood up as I reached for the recorder. She became formal and proper. "I think you both have met Mrs. Halsted. Mother, I would like you to meet Mr. Lawson from America."

As we shook hands, the judge and two attorneys arrived with their wives. They were followed by the Commissioner of Paris Police and his young wife, and the President of French Criminal Affairs who was with the United States Ambassador to France. All were dressed formally.

The judge, in his best English, said, "This is all so highly irregular. I mean, dining at six, it's so Louis the 14th."

Nancy apologized. "I am sorry, but it is most important. Time, right now is of the essence."

The waiters were called in and drinks were served. Later, they adjourned to the dinner table. As soon as the guests were seated, Nancy called for their attention. "Ladies and Gentlemen, before we dine, Mrs. Halsted has something to say to all of us. It concerns testimony she gave that sent an innocent man to be hanged."

Sarah's face showed her suffering and distress. The guests had been rendered silent by Nancy's announcement. None of them could imagine what Sarah was about to say.

Nancy broke the silence. "I know it is not proper to turn a dinner party into a courtroom, but Mrs. Sarah Halsted has a confession to make that involves a man who has been accused of something he did not do. Because of her testimony, you were all confident that justice had been done. All because Mrs. Halsted forgot to include in her testimony that she was once married to the condemned man. All because of her hate and her desire for revenge, she gave false testimony."

Everyone stared at Sarah, who saw the courage and patience in Nancy's face. She also saw deep determination. She knew she couldn't win. After a few hypocritical tears, she said, "It's all true!" She sobbed, "I lied on the witness stand!" Her crying outdid Barbara Stanwyck. "I didn't see him throw the man over the balcony. I couldn't have, I was just coming in

157

the door. But it was a chance to get even. I am ashamed and sorry. I could never live with myself knowing that I caused the death of someone."

When she made that last statement I glanced at Nancy. She looked as if she were about to become ill.

The judge stood up. "My God!" he shouted. "Do you realize what this would do to the name of justice? We must stop the execution!" Everyone nodded in agreement. The judge angrily pointed at Sarah. "You realize this is perjury?"

Sarah calmly replied, "If I didn't tell you, it would have been murder."

The judge stood speechless.

The prosecuting attorney spoke up. "Shouldn't someone call the prison?"

This led to a lengthy discussion about the proper action be taken in the case. It went on forever.

They would have speeded up if they knew what was taking place at the prison.

The warden, a short, stern man, asked over and over again, as he paced Lazarus' cell, staring at the body, "Are you sure he's dead?"

The doctor shrugged his shoulders. "Ill est mort."

"Are you sure?" demanded the warden.

"With some people around this prison you can't tell, but this man, I assure you, is dead."

"Sacre bleu!" shouted the warden.

"Don't feel so bad," suggested the doctor, "he saved you a hanging."

The warden changed his attitude. "Au contraire! He will be hung."

The doctor stood amazed. "You can't hang a dead man. Take him to the morgue," demanded the doctor.

The warden became most authoritative. "The court decreed that the prisoner was to be hanged, so he *will* hang!"

"Why, you fiendish gargoyle!" said the disgusted doctor.

"The law is the law!" shouted the warden.

158

"Please," said the monk, "have respect for the dead."

"Look," said the frustrated warden, "all I have to do is go out there and announce to that press group that there will be no hanging and I can see the headlines: AMERICAN GOES FREE. I would be mocked. They will say that the rich American bought his way out of the hangman's noose. No one will believe he died before the hanging. Oh, no, he will be hanged in one hour and ten minutes." The warden looked at his watch. "What time do you have?"

The doctor said, "One hour until midnight."

"Then he dies on time."

The doctor shook his head in disbelief. "Why, you gout, you should have every tooth removed but one. And that should be a toothache!"

At the party, I looked at my watch. They had been discussing what to do forever, and finally, after almost three hours, *had* decided to call the prison. After they had been trying to get through for several minutes without success, I suggested that they step up their efforts because the execution was only an hour away.

The Police Commissioner got on the phone. "Operator, this is Monsieur Molin, Commissioner of Police. It is important that I speak with the warden of the Paris Prison. I must speak with the warden, it has to do with an execution." There was a pause. "We'll, find him! And get him to stop the execution." There was another pause while he listened. "What do you mean, the man that was to be executed is dead?"

Nancy did all she could to prevent herself from fainting. "They executed him early?" she screamed.

The commissioner cupped his hand over the phone. "He died in his cell."

Nancy and I looked at each other.

"Then he is alive!" she shouted. "Tell them not to do anything!"

"We will be right out!" shouted the commissioner into the phone.

Mildred threw her arms around Nancy after wiping tears from her eyes. "You have taught me a lesson in faith," she sniffed. "I am so happy that your friend, Mr. Benson, is all right."

Nancy embraced her mother. "I have another surprise." She opened her purse and handed her mother the diamond ring.

"My ring!" Mildred exclaimed with surprise and joy.

"I'll explain later. There is no time now," Nancy replied.

I asked the commissioner if he had a police helicopter large enough to fly the necessary people to the prison.

"Why not," he replied, "there is a landing pad on the roof of this hotel."

"Then get it over here right away, every second counts," I commanded.

The commissioner yelled into the phone, "Tell the warden not to do a thing. We will be right out to the prison. Make all the arrangements for landing a helicopter." He then dialed headquarters and ordered the aircraft to come to the hotel's landing pad right away. 'Toute suite!"

Nancy, the commissioner, the judge, the two attorneys and the president of the Legion of Criminal Affairs all went to the roof.

I suggested that the rest of the folks all enjoy themselves. "We will return after this mess is straightened out. And someone comfort Sarah." Then I joined the others on the roof.

We boarded the craft and flew to the prison. The guards were alerted and as soon as we landed we were escorted to the scaffold. Nancy's white chiffon dress flowed as she hurried along the dreary prison halls. For a second I could experience what Lazarus saw when he returned to life.

Not far away from us, in Lazarus' cell, the warden called two guards. "Take this man to the scaffold." The guards put their arms under Lazarus' arms and carried him to the gallows.

As the onlookers made notes there was a deep silence that was broken when one man inquired, "What is wrong with the prisoner?"

160

The doctor shouted, "I am Dr. LaTwuir. I have examined the prisoner. He is dead but the warden demands that he be hanged."

A hush fell upon the crowd. It was ten minutes before twelve.

Our entourage entered the death chamber. Upon seeing the scaffold and hangman, Nancy closed her eyes and shook her head. Then she broke away from the dignitaries and ran to Lazarus. I followed her.

Nancy knelt beside his body, gently took his hand, and whispered, "Mr. Benson, come back, please come back. It's me, Nancy. Please open your eyes. Look at me!"

The monk took her by the shoulders and tried to comfort her. "Bless you child. It's too late, he's dead."

She looked up at the dear man. "No, he will resuscitate," she said most tearfully. Again, she pleaded, "It's all right. Sarah confessed. You are free. Here, hold my hand and follow me."

Suddenly there was a hush. Lazarus moved. The reporters were stunned. As Lazarus began to sit up, one of the reporters fell to his knees and folded his hands in prayer.

The monk blessed himself and stood in fear, as if he had seen the second coming. "I'll be a son of a bitch!" he said.

"Everything is all right," Nancy said, holding Lazarus' hand and using all her strength and concentration to help revive him. Then she moved back, the tension was ready to snap. Lazarus slowly opened his eyes and smiled as he saw Nancy's loveliness. Not only had the vision brought him back, but that very vision was alive and holding his hand. Lazarus stood up.

Everyone was silent. The doctor shook his stethoscope, then put the plugs in his ears and blew into the end piece, almost deafening himself. He walked away shaking his head in disbelief.

Lazarus saw me and threw his arms around me in a warm embrace. "Dear friends, you both came," he whispered.

"Yes," said Nancy, "and you are free. Sarah confessed that she lied."

He embraced us both at the same time.

The judge walked up to Lazarus with tears in his eyes and kissed him on both cheeks. "I am so sorry that I was the one who put you through this unforgettable trauma. Such an injustice! This is a miracle."

The President of Criminal Affairs shook Lazarus' hand. "Forgive such blind justice. But when someone lies so convincingly on the witness stand, who knows?"

"It's all right," assured Lazarus. "It takes courage to live these days. Crime lurks everywhere. We all must pretend we are wearing invisible armor."

I turned to the press. "Ladies and Gentlemen, I am Jim Lawson, a newsman from America. I am sure one of these gentlemen has a statement to make."

The Commissioner of Police stepped forward as if he were making a formal political speech. "Honorable Judge LaFab, Messrs. President of the French Legion of Criminal Affairs, Prosecuting Attorney, Lawyer Dubois, Warden Flaber, and Ladies and Gentlemen of the Press, after careful police investigation and diligent work, we uncovered a fraud. A Mrs. Sarah Halsted perjured herself on the witness stand, gave false testimony that this man, her ex-husband, threw a man over the balcony of a ten story hotel, and did this with malice aforethought. Her testimony brought the death sentence to an innocent man. After a quick inquiry this man will be free and within twelve hours he will be able to grant you all interviews."

Nancy and Lazarus walked out through the dark prison halls.

The next day the headlines shouted in praise of a miracle. One week later, Lazarus was the main attraction at the Paris Opera House. Then he was booked all over Europe, playing to standing room only.

The Great Lazarus, by dying, was again making an honest living.